This book is dedicated to my family, the ones I was born with and the ones I've collected on the way. The only people I want to spend Christmas with. I love you. Now kindly refrain from reading any further

This is intended as a fun Christmas Romance but the fun is of the adult variety. Therefore, please note that this book is not suitable for people under 18.

Before reading, please consider, the following content warnings:

- Fat shaming
- Bereavement
- Family Drama

And A Partridge on Pear Street

H.R. Lloyd

CHAPTER ONE
"Yeah, this is the place."

NEL

My Uber pulls up outside my brother's home. It's a two-storey, brick building with wisteria vines climbing the façade. Toward the end of December, there are no flowers aside from the large wreath hung on the door, adorned with deep red poinsettias and velvet ribbon. The driveway is big enough for ten Smart Cars or seven normal sized cars, and the house is double the width of the one we grew up in.

"This the right place?" my driver asks awkwardly.

I may have been sat staring for a couple of minutes, trying to gather up my courage and Christmas cheer for the onslaught to come. Hey, I got my nails done in a nice holly-berry red with glittering white snowflakes painted on each one. How much more Christmas spirit can one have? I sigh, "Yeah, this is the place."

Tipping the guy and collecting my suitcase from the boot, I make my way to the front door, the iffy wheel of my case making it difficult to navigate. One more big breath of cold air to settle the nerves flitting about in the pit of my stomach and I knock on the holly-green door. It swings open with some force and a man I kind of recognise beams at me from behind a thick grey moustache.

"Penelope!" His booming voice can probably be heard throughout Pear Street.

"Hi." My voice comes out smaller than I would like, and I give a dorky wave as I try and remember this guy's name. This is my sister-in-law's father, I'm pretty sure...or maybe her uncle? They look very similar.

"Come on in, duck." He opens the door wider and steps aside. It's her dad, I remember from the wedding that he likes to call people duck. Weird, if you ask me.

"Thanks." I offer a polite smile and haul my suitcase over the threshold. He takes it from me and wheels it to a corner out of the way. Before I know what's happening, he wraps me in a giant hug, tighter than I find comfortable, and he kisses my cheek, his grey bristles tickling me.

"Your brother is in the kitchen." He pats my shoulder, his broad smile still in place as he ushers me down the hall.

The wide hallway is adorned with lush looking green garlands winding through the spindles of the staircase. There are foil snowflakes hanging from the tall ceiling and I spot a huge, live tree as I pass the lounge. Not like the old plastic one Dad used to haul out of the attic every December. There are decorations everywhere, none of them tacky or over the top. *Shouldn't there be a little tack at Christmas?*

The bright kitchen is also decorated. *Is it normal to put Christmas decorations in the kitchen?* It's chock-a-block with people. *Jesus.* I'm so thankful that I have a hotel room and can escape this bustle at the end of each day while I'm required to endure this picture-perfect family Christmas. It is lightyears away from the family Christmases I'm used to. Without warning, pain lances through my chest as I remember why I'm here and not where I have spent the previous twenty-eight Christmases. I swallow down the thickness in my throat as my brother comes into view with a smile painted on his handsome face. The tightness around his eyes belies his ease.

"Nelly-Belly," he greets, his smile becoming more genuine as he slings an arm around my shoulders.

"Hey, Harry. How are you doing?" I give him a gentle squeeze.

2

"Oh, just fine. Lisa's whole family is here so I'm just trying to keep everyone's drinks topped up and smiles on faces while I dodge the inevitable '*I'm sorry about your parents*' pity stare."

I wince and my hand goes to my chest to rub the heartache away. Harry gives me a small sympathetic smile.

"Just smile and nod. They'll all say it once, then you can move on."

I nod. It was hard losing Dad in January, but he'd been ill for a while. We knew last Christmas would be our last with him, so we made sure to spend as much time with him as we could, making memories to hold on to when he'd gone. We just didn't realise it would be Mum's last one too. After cancer finally took Dad, Mum just shut down; she was never the same. When summer came, so did her chest pain. We took her to doctors and specialists but no one could find anything wrong until it was too late. *Takotsubo cardiomyopathy*, also known as broken heart syndrome. That's what they told us when they patted our arms and apologised for our loss.

So here I am, spending Christmas at my brother's big expensive house with him and his perfect family and his wife's oversized extended family. I'm so far out of my comfort zone that I can't even see the zone anymore. It's not that I don't like people, I do, it's just that I prefer them on a one-on-one setting. Lots of people in one place is so overwhelming that I find myself unable to join in conversations easily or enjoy myself. I was told I come across rude when I shut down—by my brother, at Mum's funeral. That's why I need the hotel. It'll give me a chance to recharge my social battery at the end of each day.

"Hey, thanks for staying at the hotel," Harry says. "Lisa feels really bad we didn't have room for everyone, but with her mum helping out so much and her uncle's hip replacement, it was better for them to stay here. Plus her cousin has the kids, it would be awkward for them travelling back and forth every day—"

"Harry," I place my hand on his arm lightly. "It's really okay. I'll feel better at the hotel, I can get out of everyone's way." This was the best part. Harry and Lisa thought I was doing *them* a favour. My brother would probably be mortally offended if I admitted that I wanted to get away from them at the end of each day. "At least this way you don't have to cater to me twenty-four-seven."

Harry laughs and pokes a finger into my soft belly. "Like I can afford to keep you fed twenty-four hours a day."

Great. Nice Harry lasted all of three minutes. Unfortunately, only one of us was blessed with the best parts of our parents. Harry is tall like Dad was, with sandy blonde hair like Mum's. His green eyes are hers, too, but his metabolism is Dad's. The two of them could eat whatever they want, whenever they want, and stay lean and toned. Mum used to say that she only had to look at a slice of cake and she'd gain two pounds, and I'm exactly the same. No matter what diets or work out regimens I try, I can never lose my big belly, flabby arms, or thighs of thunder. I always start strong, losing big numbers in the first few weeks, then I plateau regardless of how strict I am with myself. After a particularly tough time of dieting a few years ago where I'd got to the point of nearly starving myself, I made a very conscious decision that I didn't want to waste another moment of my life denying myself just to seek approval from others. I worked hard on loving my curves and embracing my natural figure, and after a while I became comfortable in the skin I'm in. Well, most of the time. Harry has an uncanny ability to tear down the confidence I've built. I love my brother and I know he loves me; he just never grew out of the big brother teasing stage of siblinghood.

"Come on, Nelly-Belly, let's go say hi to everyone."

I feel like I'm in a cramming revision session as Harry reintroduces me to all his in-laws. Lisa's father, who had let me in, sits at the large dining table with his wife. I'm reminded of their names, Charles and Camilla. *I shit you not.* How did I forget that? With them is Charles' brother Gordan and his wife Hen. Gordan looks exactly like Charles—tall and broad, white haired, and blue eyed—luckily Gordan is clean shaven so I should be able to tell them apart easily. What's weird though is that their wives also look similar. Camilla is petite and delicate with blonde hair streaked with white, her light brown eyes are warm and kind, and her smile bright and genuine. Hen has a similar build but her hair a light brown colour with not a grey in sight. She also has brown eyes and a joyful expression. Hen and Gordan's daughter, Rhiannon, and her husband Luke are in the kitchen, too, but constantly on the move chasing after their twins, Margot and Freddie.

Everyone is friendly and seems genuinely pleased to see me. A wave of panic hits me. What if I disappoint them when I'm not a great conversationalist or when I don't have any funny jokes or anecdotes to tell? *It's okay, Nel. One day at a time. Get through the next few hours and then you can soak in the bath of your hotel room where no one can talk at you or ask questions.*

Swallowing back my nerves, I am just giving everyone the smile I'd practiced when Lisa comes bustling into the kitchen. My sister-in-law is one of those annoyingly perfect human beings. She's beautiful with blonde hair that always cascades in perfectly formed wavy curls, naturally slim with big boobs and curvy hips. Although right now her usual figure is hidden by a giant baby bump. She still has two months to go and I can't imagine her getting any bigger without toppling over. Even without the stunning good looks, she's enviable. A human rights solicitor, culinary wizard, black belt in karate, and President of the Parent Teacher Association. All this while raising two—soon to be three—kids, living with my brother, and maintaining a permanently immaculate house. To top it all off, she's so bloody lovely, it's sickening. I hate her a little bit.

"Nel!" She comes at me with arms open for a hug and I succumb to her embrace, somewhat stiffly. It's not her, I'm just not a touchy-feely kind of person. It's weird because my parents were always very affectionate with us, and Harry is with his family. I used to be, but I just hate people touching me. I always

5

feel so…*big* in someone else's arms. That feeling is magnified by the fact that Lisa's arms barely get round my shoulders as she has to hug around the giant beachball under her festive jumper.

"Hi, Lisa."

"How's my favourite sister-in-law?" She releases me only to hold me at arms'—and belly's—length.

"I'm your only sister-in-law," I remind her and any further attempt to answer her question is thwarted by the scene coming in to view behind her.

My two nephews are squealing and squawking in utter delight, each one hanging off the bicep of the most beautiful man I've ever known. One I was *not* expecting to see here. One whose name was on nearly every page of the glittery, pink, padlocked diary I kept as a teenager. One I haven't spoken to in years and one who happens to be Harry's best friend.

CHAPTER TWO
"Umm…what are you having?"

NEL

Jake Partridge shuffles into the kitchen from the hall, taking over exaggerated steps, swinging the delighted boys as they cling to his curled-up arms. He's in a soft looking, grey V-neck sweater and dark jeans, his dark brown hair combed back with a couple of strands artfully curling forward over his brow. His jaw is lined in a dark but well-kept beard. That's new. I try to swallow over the dryness in my throat. This is a nightmare I have not prepared for. He grunts with each step as though he's struggling with their weight but the easy smile on his face tells a different story.

Lucas, my oldest nephew spots me first and turns to me with a gapped tooth smile. "Hi Auntie Nelly-Belly!" So glad Harry taught them that. My eyes are rolling if you didn't pick up on that sarcasm.

Jake snaps his head up to look at me, hitting me with his signature smile. You know those old clips of a young Elvis? The ones where he gives a half smile, one so shyly confident it made panties wet and women (as well as a few men, I'm sure) would just melt into a pile of aroused goo? Yeah. That's the smile that Jake Partridge perfected when he was thirteen years old and he's been ruining women everywhere with it ever since. His honey-golden eyes, so full of laughter and mischief, lock on mine. As though I hadn't already been awkward and nervous around my sister-in-law's family, I turn into teen Penelope. Braces, acne, and foundation two shades darker than my actual skin tone. Stood in front of the guitar playing, rugby superstar with the

7

kilowatt smile who always had a pretty girl hanging on his every word.

I stand there staring at him gormlessly and he chuckles slightly like he knows. Of course, he knows. I was a loser fat kid with close to no friends and zero chill. It would have been almost impossible for him to miss the humungous crush I harboured for him for years. I'd love to be able to say that I'm now a smart, confident woman who doesn't hold on to silly school-girl crushes and can quite easily greet Jake Partridge as an old friend. I would just *love* to.

"Hey, Nelly-Belly," he says with that smooth as chocolate voice, calming and thrilling at the same time. I try and fail to tamp down my wince at him using that name.

"Uh…Jake…what are…what are you doing here?" I squeak.

"Jeesh, Nels," Harry mutters next to me. "Rude much?" He narrows his eyes at me in the oh-so-familiar way he used to when we were kids. I swear, sometimes he believes he's my parent, not my brother. "Jake's only my best friend of twenty-four years, spent nearly every Saturday at our house, best man at my wedding, and Godfather to both my kids. Don't you think he's earned the right to spend Christmas here without you questioning why?" Harry's glower is nearly as scary as Mum's was, I'll give him that.

"I'm sorry…I didn't mean—"

"It's fine, H. Give the poor girl a break." Jake deposits the boys and approaches me with a wide smile, pulling me into a bear-hug that clamps my arms to my side. Oh God. Make it stop. "Long time no see, Nel. How the hell are you, kid?"

My parents are dead and now I'm surrounded by a load of people I don't know and my childhood crush who I can't function around for Christmas. Oh yeah, I'm great.

"I'm good, Jake. How are you?"

"I'm perfect," he beams at me. *You sure are.*

I'm still confused as to why he's here but I don't want to risk another scolding from my brother, so I tuck a piece of my overly long brown hair behind my ear and look to the ground as I ask, "So how come you're not spending Christmas with your folks?"

"Ah, they're in Australia spending Christmas with my sister and the grandkids. I couldn't get enough time off to make the trip worth it so I'm gate-crashing the Forrest Christmas celebrations." He casually slides his hands into the pockets of his jeans, bringing my attention to his thick forearms, tanned gold with a light dusting of dark hair. If PornHub created a forearm porn category, Jake Partridge could make a fortune.

I nod, trying to shake my gaze free of his annoyingly sexy arm hair. Pushing distractions away, I process what he's just said. "Don't teachers get two weeks off at Christmas?"

"We do," he smiles a cocky smile, like he's enjoying some private joke, and it brings a flush to my face. "But I'm also a volunteer firefighter and I'll be working over New Years."

Of course, he's a volunteer firefighter. Because Jake Partridge is fucking perfect. "Oh."

His smile widens as my cheeks pinken, but drops quite suddenly as he clears his throat, glancing to my boots. "Hey, I'm really sorry about your mum, Nel. Your dad too, obviously. I just know Mary's passing was unexpected."

A lump the size of a golf ball forms in my throat and tears sting at the back of my eyes as I try to think of anything else that will stop them from overflowing, nodding my head at his words. I try for a polite smile but I know it looks as forced as it feels.

"I was at both funerals, I'm sure you know, but I wasn't able to catch you to talk."

"No," I croak, trying to clear my throat. "I uh, well I wasn't really in a social mood,"

He tilts his head and offers a soft and sympathetic smile. "That's understandable."

I look up at him to see the sincerity in his eyes. My brother had thrown a fit when he'd found me in a ball of pity inside my mother's walk-in wardrobe during her wake. To be fair, I did feel guilty for leaving him to all the mourners. I just couldn't take all the arm pats and sympathetic gazes, people telling me how wonderful my mother was as if I didn't know that already. Each cheek pinch or forced hug was another weight on my shoulder until I could barely walk and I had to get away. Apparently, Harry had been looking for me for an hour when he finally came up to Mum's room and found me. I got a spiel about responsibility and representing the family and how he and I were supposed to be a team. I had just sat there nodding my head as I cried. It was all pretty pathetic. I'm glad Jake didn't witness me like that.

"Is it?" I ask remembering Harry telling me the complete opposite.

Jake glances at my brother quickly, as if he knows my thoughts, before stepping slightly closer and lowering his voice to a gentle assurance. "Yeah, it is. There are no set rules on how to deal with grief, Nel. Everyone needs different things and if you needed to be away from other people, I'm certainly not going to hold it against you."

My throat is clogged with emotion again and all I can manage is another nod. He is close enough now that I can smell him, something aromatic like allspice and citrus. Jake always smelled nice, something familiar and homey but it seemed to change slightly with the seasons. Summer holidays were spent drenched in the scent of sun cream and something uniquely green, like fresh cut grass. And winters were the smell of bonfires with that same spice and orange that fills my nostrils now. I can feel my cheeks heating as I try to think of anything but the inexplicable craving I have to bury my nose in his neck and sniff him like a line of coke. Luckily, I can always rely on my nephews to take a situation from awkward to downright mortifying.

"Hey, Auntie Nel, do you have a boyfriend yet?" Lucas asked, playing with the end of my scarf that I'm still wearing. "Dad says you've never had one."

Kill me now.

"I didn't say that!" Harry bursts out and Jake chuckles. I feel a little stifled as I note that everyone in the kitchen is watching this exchange about my love life, or lack of. Of course, I realise I'm still wearing my hat, scarf, and coat like I'm about to bolt out the door. *Now there's an idea.*

"Lucas, stop being rude," Lisa admonishes.

"How am I being rude?" he argues, throwing his hands in the air with the attitude of a teenager; a bit premature at nine years old. If I wasn't trying so hard to avoid everyone's eyes, I probably would have found time to find it funny.

"Asking someone if they have a boyfriend or girlfriend yet is rude. Now stop arguing and ask Auntie Nel if she'd like a drink." Lisa looks down at her eldest with what can only be describes as *The Look*: the one all mums can muster and warns children against arguments.

Lucas huffs and turns to me with a scowl. "Would you like a drink?"

Is it okay to ask an nine-year-old for alcohol? Asking for a friend.

"We have red, white, and rosé," Lisa offers, "Vodka, gin, whiskey, amaretto, coke, lemonade, tonic. Or we can do a cocktail. I can make a snowball, amaretto sour, or Cosmo."

I blink at her. "Err...cocktail?"

"Sure, which one?" She smiles warmly, not at all showing how irritating my answer is.

"Umm...what are you having?" I know that is the stupidest question as soon as it's out of my lips and I close my eyes to shield from the embarrassment.

"I'm on lime and soda," she says cheerily, again ignoring my utter incompetence at human-ing today. I hear Jake chuckle and I just want to die.

"Amaretto sour would be great," I say with a forced smile.

"Sure," she beams. "Come on, terror." She says, turning to Lucas. "Let me show you how to make a decent cocktail."

The two of them head toward the garage where I know Harry and Lisa have a cocktail bar and I feel a tug at my coat. Looking down, I find Oscar looking back up at me. Now, I know parents are not meant to choose a favourite child, that makes perfect sense to me. But does the rule apply for Aunties too? Don't get me wrong, I love Lucas. But he's such a…kid. He's loud and excitable, he asks quickfire questions that I usually have no idea how to answer, and he tells long winded stories with sound effects that I struggle to keep up with. It's not his fault—he's perfect—I'm just not really great with kids, and Lucas is the ultimate kid. Oscar, however, is quiet and calm. I don't see the boys all that often but when I do, Oscar and I are like kindred spirits. We often end up in a corner somewhere, soaking in quiet company, him reading while I check my phone, and I may be biased but he's seriously cute.

"Hi Aunty Nels-Bells," he whispers.

"Hi Ozzy," I smile at him.

"Why are you still wearing your coat?" he asks softly, gently stroking my camel wool coat.

"I forgot to take it off," I answer honestly, and he giggles at me.

"That's silly."

"Here," Jake steps forward, holding his hand out. "I'll take it."

I unbutton my coat and shrug out of it, Jake's eyes dart to my chest and away again just as quick, and for what feels like the thousandth time within ten minutes, I blush when I notice my shirt gaping where the buttons strain over my breasts. Quickly adjusting the offending garment, I cover myself back up and pull my bobble hat and scarf off too, finger combing my loose curls to get rid of hat-hair. Jake gives me a tight smile before taking the items into the hall. Great. I've probably made him feel uncomfortable. No one wants their best friend's little sister flashing them a peek of her purple satin bra.

"Guys," Lisa says, emerging from the garage with my drink in hand and Lucas in tow. "We can all start getting up to the table now. The salad is ready!"

Salad? How festive.

CHAPTER THREE
"What kind of Photography?"

JAKE

Penelope Forrest has grown up. I mean I caught glimpses of her twice this year at her parents' funerals, but she was obviously not up for conversations. I still remember her drawn expression and blotchy, red face. I'd wanted to wrap her up in a hug and stroke her hair. Little Nel, Harry's baby sister, the girl I grew up with, who used to blush every time I smiled at her, and who held her head down when she walked in public. I hated to see her tears, I always had. Before the funerals, I probably hadn't seen Nel for about five years, not in person anyway. I had definitely seen all the pictures she's been posting online. *Wait, does that sound stalkerish?*

It's not like she was a kid when I last spent any time with her. She was fresh out of university and although I'd noticed a slight change from the girl I'd once known, she was still curled in on herself as she sat and avoided eye contact with everyone. She used to wear baggy clothes and big cardigans even in the height of summer, but she has changed. In blue skinny jeans and knee-high, tan, leather boots and a satin blouse that hugs her chest, the first few buttons undone to show more cleavage than she ever would before. Then she went and took her coat off and flashed me her sexy as fuck bra; deep purple with black lace trimming the cups. It was visible all of one second, but that image is now seared into my retinas. Of course, it's nothing compared to the images of her from social media that live rent-free in my brain. They're definitely not the images that should come to mind when one thinks of their best friend's little sister.

I hang her coat, hat, and scarf up on the hooks in the hall, getting a whiff of her brown sugar and cinnamon smell. I check the corridor quickly thinking of burying my nose in her coat and inhaling hard, but I manage to refrain. I freakin' love that smell. I hear Lisa call everyone up to the table and head back into the kitchen where the only seat available is next to Cami, Lisa's mother. Sliding in between her and Rhiannon, I offer them both a smile and detangle the green napkin on my plate that's been elegantly folded to look like an elf's hat. Nel is sat opposite me, with Charles and Gordon on either side. She seems to tuck herself in, hands in her lap and shoulders curled over, studying her plate like it holds all the answers, and not making eye contact with anyone. She's far more recognisable as the girl I once knew like this, not the girl I'm dying to get to know, who posts those photos on Instagram.

Harry and Lisa have a big, beautiful house, and their kitchen-diner is spacious. But even with the table extended as far as it will go, it's a squeeze with twelve chairs and two highchairs. Still, everyone is smiling and laughing as Lisa brings out a huge platter laden with slices of delicious smelling ham.

"Darling, I told you I would carry that in!" Harry jumps up to help his wife, taking the dish from her while shaking his head in gentle admonishment.

"Please, I'm pregnant. Not incapable," she protests with a smile on her face.

Everyone oohs and aahs as Harry lays the giant plate down on the middle of the table, and the smell of roasted honey and meat wafts around us. Nel's eyes widen in surprise when the dish is set in front of her.

"This looks incredible, Lisa," she says, offering a shy smile to our hostess.

"Well, thank you, hon." Lisa's returning smile is much wider as she slides into her seat in that way pregnant women do.

Harry ropes the boys in to help him and slowly but surely the table fills up.

"I thought you said we were having salad, sweetheart." Cami laughs by my side.

"Well, it's Christmas, salad is a bit plain, we had to jazz it up a bit."

A gargantuan bowl of salad is the second showstopper to be placed on the table. Adorned with cranberries, pomegranates, pistachios, and red onions that look to have been pickled, all laid on a bed of deep green leaves. It looks very festive. As soon as Harry takes his place at the head of the table, opposite Lisa, and motions for us to dig in, there are hands everywhere. I'm passed the basket of bread and the salad servers before passing them to Rhiannon, but she's busy wrestling her son into a bib. So I serve her a portion while her back is turned and pass her husband the implements to serve himself. I watch as Nel slides a thick slice of ham onto her plate and butters her roll with a heavy hand before piling the salad on top of her meat. She catches me staring and immediately looks back down at her plate, her cheeks turning red.

Conversation starts easily and everyone chats as old friends, except Nel who stays quiet, eyes darting between people as they speak. She seems to enjoy her food though, her first bite has her eyes rolling to the back of her head and she puts her hand over her mouth as she chews, nodding to herself as though agreeing with her tastebuds that it's delicious. My cock notices, twitching in my jeans while I watch her eat. *Okay, stop being a perv, Partridge, there are children around, for fuck's sake.*

"Oh!" Lisa says, suddenly, getting up from her chair and fetching something from the kitchen counter. "Jake, Nel, you guys got here a bit later so you haven't had your itineraries yet." She hands us each an A4 sheet of paper with lots of typed writing on it.

At a quick glance, I can see a plan for the next few days, each item with a specific timeslot. Looking across the table I stifle my chuckle as Nel stares at the paper with horror.

"Obviously, the itinerary starts tomorrow, Christmas Eve-Eve, so tonight is a bit of a free for all," Lisa chuckles.

"How devil-may-care of you Lis," I smirk at her, and she sticks her tongue out at me in response.

"Mummy!" Lucas gasps at her action.

"That was an adult necessity, it doesn't give you permission to do it." Lisa narrows her eyes at her son, but her smirk tells him she's just playing. This causes both her boys to giggle.

"Umm…" Nel speaks up and the whole table quietens, probably because it's the first thing she's said since we sat down. "Did Harry tell you I need to head back to the city on Christmas Eve, for work?"

Lisa waves at her dismissively. "Of course, hon. You do what you've got to do. You can check with the itinerary so you'll know where we are when you get back and you can catch up with us."

"Remind me what you do for work, Penelope," Charles asks, taking a break from shovelling food into his face and dabbing his moustache with his napkin.

Harry clears his throat and shuffles in his seat. "Uh, Charles, can you pass me the bread please?"

Charles does as he's asked but looks over to Nel expectantly. "I'm a photographer," she says with a nod.

My lips twitch. Harry has never been particularly keen on Nel's choice of subject when she went pro with her photography, but it wasn't until she got in front of the camera that he became downright disapproving. I suppress my smile at the memory of Harry and I at our weekly squash game when he arrived in a bad mood, huffing and puffing until I finally asked him what was wrong. When he told me that Nel, his sweet and shy baby sister, was posting photos of herself in lingerie on Instagram, I think he was expecting me to be as disgusted as he was. Not for me to just shrug and suggest we start the game. He most definitely wasn't expecting—and will never know—how quickly I searched her name online, found her account, and looked at the posts in question.

Nel is a boudoir photographer with a small studio in London. She promotes her business heavily on social media and in just a couple of years, she has blown up in popularity. From what I've gathered—by what a professional might call my *stalking*—she had a client who was nervous to pose in her underwear, so Nel decided to strip with her. They took a selfie and Nel posted it on her page to show there was nothing to be afraid of. Since then, she started doing posing tutorials on TikTok in an effort to boost women's confidence while wearing lingerie just as she suggests others do. She also does makeup tutorials and fashion posts. From there, she started getting sponsorships from lingerie companies and I have been following her avidly—What can I say? She has charisma—She's definitely the most famous person I know.

"Oh splendid!" Charles exclaims, placing his drink on the table. "What kind of photography? Weddings?"

"No, it can't be weddings," Cami laughed. "Otherwise, she would have photographed Lisa and Harry's wedding."

"Nel was still in university when Lis got married," Rhiannon told her with an amused smile. Nel shuffled awkwardly in her seat. "Us bridesmaids had plenty of time to chat while the bride was flapping over things that didn't need flapping over and I distinctly remember her saying she was at university studying art and photography, right?" She narrows her eyes and points across to Nel in question.

Nel smiles politely and nods.

"Hey, I did not flap over things," Lisa protests.

"My darling, I love you dearly, but you were the flappiest of flappy brides," Harry says, leaning back in his chair with his wine in hand.

"Oh pish, if I flapped, it was only because you were so annoyingly calm about everything." She flicked her wrist at him.

"I had no reason to be anything but calm, I was marrying the perfect woman." He smiles lovingly down the table and when I catch his eye, I make sure to mime a small gag, to which he rubs his eye with his middle finger in my direction.

"Well, that's all very lovely," Gordan rolls his eyes. "But we were learning about Penelope."

"Oh, please," Nel says quietly. "Call me Nel."

"Yeah, she's Auntie Nelly-Belly," Lucas says with a big, toothy—and slightly gappy—grin.

"Nelly-Belly?" Charles asks, laughing at his grandson.

"My little Nelly-Belly," Harry smiles at his sister, affectionately.

She gives a slightly tighter smile back. *Man*, for someone who can be so open and self-assured online, Nel really hates talking about herself.

"So," Hen, says gently. "What kind of photographer are you, sweetie?"

I watch Harry try to give Nel the eye, a warning not to reveal too much, but she's too focussed on her plate, tucking a strand of light-brown hair behind her ear.

"I mostly do portraits," she says. "I have a studio in the city."

"Oh fabulous," Cami beams. "Do you do family portraits? Maybe we should all come along and do a shoot?" She asks, looking between her husband, daughter, and son-in-law.

Harry's eyes widen in terror as I choke on my sip of wine. I cough and splutter, banging on my chest with a closed fist. Rhiannon pats my back in concern and Nel stares at me like a deer in headlights.

"I'm sure Nel doesn't have time for that," Harry stutters.

I catch Nel narrowing her eyes at her brother before lifting her chin and smiling at Cami. "I'd be happy to do some family photos for you. But the studio is too small for a large group, so we could look at some cool outdoor spaces for you."

"That sounds wonderful," Cami beams, completely satisfied with that.

Because Harry tends to get a little uptight around his in-laws, and because I'm a sucker for a bit of awkwardness—plus come on, it's Christmas, we all deserve a little fun—I decide to wind my best friend up a bit. "It's not just photography though, is it Nel? Aren't you some kind of influencer too?"

CHAPTER FOUR
"How exactly do you influence people to buy things?"

JAKE

Everyone snaps their attention to Nel, waiting for her to answer. She gapes at me, Harry glares, I just smile into the rim of my wine glass.

"Err…well…" Nel splutters, her blush colouring her cheeks and down her neck. "I mean, I guess you could say that."

"No way!" Luke says excitedly while wiping sticky toddler fingers with a baby wipe. "A real-life influencer, that's cool."

"What kind of things do you post about?" Rhiannon asks around a mouthful of salad.

"Fashion," Harry answers for his sister quickly.

"Yeah," Nel nods along. "Fashion mostly, makeup, that sort of thing."

"I was going to say your makeup is flawless," Rhiannon chomps out around a rather large chunk of bread. "I wish I had time to do something like that in the morning," she admires, pointing at Nel's face. I wouldn't have said she was wearing much on her face. Some sure, I know that the thick black line above her lashes isn't natural, but she looks perfect, not caked in the stuff like some of the teenagers I teach wear.

"Um, well, it doesn't take all that long," Nel mumbles shyly.

"So, do you get like, free stuff?" Luke asks.

"Occasionally."

"I'm sorry, I'm going to have to show my age and ask, what is an influencer exactly?" Hen asks.

"Mum," Rhiannon groans, rolling her eyes. "An influencer is someone who has a large following on social media and influences people to buy stuff from companies that sponsor them."

"Oh," Hen raises her brows and nods as though impressed. "How exactly do you influence people to buy things?"

Nel is now squirming in her seat, totally uncomfortable with everyone watching her, and I watch as her cheeks flame red. "I uh…take photos with them…or, or maybe do a video about them and tell people what I think. Um, sometimes companies give me special discount codes to give my followers so they can buy products at lower prices."

"Hm, that sounds interesting," Charles says. "Show us some of these posts then, let's see the magic happen."

Harry jumps up from his seat and claps his hands once, very loudly. "Right, who's up for dessert?"

"People are still eating their dinner, babe," Lisa frowns at him.

"Ah, well maybe another round of drinks?" Harry bounces nervously.

"There's wine on the table," Lisa counters. "Sit down, babe. Everyone is fine."

"Speaking of the wine," Cami says, picking up a bottle of the red. "This is lovely, darling. Where did you get it?"

Conversation soon gets settled on wines, then Gordan and Hen's trip around the vineyards of California. Harry relaxes back down in his chair, gulping wine from his glass. Once he is sure everyone is engaged in conversation, he glares at me and mouths, very distinctly *I'm going to kill you*. I just tip my glass back at him and gave him a wink.

"Jacob, how are things in the world of education?" Charles asks me.

"They're good thanks. Busy and never a dull day."

"Remind us, what do you teach?" Cami asks.

"English. I wanted to do Physical Education but my parents said that P.E. teachers never get promoted to headmaster, so they convinced me to go for one of the big three."

"The big three?" Luke asks, hauling a fussy Margot from her highchair and holding her to his chest, but she only wants to get down. With a huff, he lets her down to run around the table, which only causes her brother to whine and kick until he, too, is free to roam.

"Maths, English, and Science," Nel answers for me, looking surprised at her own voice.

"That's right," I smile at her, revelling at her blush blooming darker. I swear the longer she sits there, the more she's reverting back to the shy schoolgirl I used to know.

Small hands slap at my thigh before Freddie runs around to the other side of the table giggling. I gasp in feigned shock, only making him laugh more. Margot then decides to have a go and before you know it, we have two hysterical toddlers running circles around the table trying to tap my legs before I can grab their adorable little hands. Most of the adults are chuckling at the little ones, joining in here and there, trying to grab them on their way round, and generally just enjoying the pandemonium. Nel is not laughing; she watches curiously, hunched in on herself. She seems to shuffle in her seat every time one of the children passes, like she's trying to give them more room even though her chair doesn't move.

"I'll hold him down!" Lucas shrieks, running over to me and grabbing my wrists and holding them behind the back of the chair.

"No, no, no," I pretend to struggle against his hold.

Oscar snorts behind his hand watching with delight as the two smaller ones come over to tickle me to death. I groan as though I'm being tortured and the kids eat it up, laughing until no sound is actually coming out and their limbs seem to lose function.

"Okay, okay," Rhiannon cuts in. "I think we should leave poor Uncle Jake alone now."

"Please," I beg, fake snivelling. "Listen to your mother, let me live!"

Lucas giggles behind me and the twins continue their game.

"Oi, little terrors! Leave the poor man alone," Luke gets up from his seat to gather up his children, trying to manoeuvre them back into their respective chairs. They aren't having any of it until Lisa stands and asks if they want ice cream. Both of them are eager to get back seated with bibs on instantly.

"Best serve the kids some quickly before Nelly-Belly eats it all, homemade ice cream is her favourite," Harry says giving wide eyes to the kids. Lucas and Oscar giggle. Nel examines her empty plate and doesn't laugh with them. I frown at her obvious discomfort and more so at the fact that Harry doesn't seem to notice at all.

Lisa starts stacking plates and I jump up to help her, Nel does the same, collecting everyone's dirty dishes. Harry makes himself busy topping up people's drinks and refilling the water jugs on the table.

"Oh, you don't have to do that," Lisa says as I open the dishwasher.

"Don't be silly," I say. "You've made this lovely dinner, least I can do is tidy up a bit." I kiss her cheek and catch Nel watching me, but she quickly turns to start placing plates in the dishwasher.

"Why some pretty little thing hasn't snatched you up yet, I have no idea," Lisa sighs wistfully heading back out to the garage, I assume to get the ice cream from the freezer.

I chuckle, helping to tidy the dishes away and collecting the platter along with other bits from the table, before putting the leftovers in the fridge. After I wash the platter by hand, dry it up, and place it back where it belongs in a cupboard in the kitchen island, I notice Nel watching me curiously.

"You certainly know your way around this place," Nel says, closing the dishwasher.

"Yeah, well I'm here more than I'm at my own place," I laugh. "Well, at least it seems that way sometimes."

"Why?" she asks, screwing her face up in confusion.

"Harry is my best friend, I enjoy his and Lisa's company, I babysit for them regularly, and I don't like living alone." I don't really mean to say the last one and I try to brush it off by clearing my throat.

"You don't?" she asks, tilting her head.

I stand in front of her, closer than I thought I was, my expression serious for the first time tonight. "Not particularly. It gets lonely," I shrug.

Her lips twitch. "It's hard to imagine Jake Partridge lonely. Always surrounded by people, by *girls*."

She's right. In school I usually had friends with me everywhere I went, and I didn't go longer than a week without a girlfriend. Although none of them stuck around longer than a month or two at a time. It's true that I get fidgety in my own company for too long but there are only a few people whose company I enjoy for extended periods. Harry is my best friend and his wife is great, but I have never had a meaningful romantic relationship. Ever. I get suckered into the bubble of new romance; I love the cosiness of intimacy when you're just getting to know somebody. That brief period where you want to spend every waking moment with them, I love it. But once that's worn off, I get bored and irritable with sharing my time with someone. No one has ever held my interest, nor have they remained interested in me.

"Jake?" Nel's gentle voice pulls me from my musings.

"Sorry, lost in thought," I shake my head.

"Well, I'm sorry you feel lonely sometimes."

I huff a laugh, "I'm fine, it was just a comment. I'm not crying into my cereal every morning."

She smiles shyly, looking down before meeting my eye. "Well, I have three housemates, so if you ever need company—

25

"Penelope Forrest," I smirk at her, stepping closer so we're only a few inches apart and lowering my voice as though we are sharing a secret conversation. "Are you suggesting a secret rendezvous in the city?"

Her eyes widen in panic and her whole face flames red. "No! I mean…what? I didn't mean…you know? I was just trying…b-b-because you're Harry's best friend and we've known each other since forever, so you're kind of my friend too…I guess…and I was just trying to…be nice…I—"

I laugh, "Oh, Nelly-Belly, you're too easy." I put my arm over her shoulders and lead her back to the table as Lisa emerges with a tray holding an ice cream tub, some sauces, sprinkles, and other accoutrement.

Harry jumps up again to take the tray from his wife at the last minute and puts it down on the table. Everyone makes lip-smacking noises as Lisa makes everyone a sundae, personalised to their individual orders. The boys want extra-large with extra everything. Rhiannon asks that the twins get a single scoop with no adornments, but Luke keeps sharing his sprinkles with them when his wife's back is turned.

Nel declines dessert and Harry pretends to faint in his seat with shock, which makes everyone laugh. The boys join in, copying their father with delirious giggles until Lisa quietly tells them enough is enough. The ice cream is delicious and I gorge myself until my stomach feels stretched beyond comfort, but hey, that's what Christmas is about.

"Well," Lisa says once everyone is finished. "I have not made any plans for this evening so it's a free for all."

"Let's play a game," Lucas suggests.

"You and your brother are off to bed now," Lisa says with quiet authority.

"Why do we have to go to bed before the babies?" he complains.

Lisa pointedly stares at the little ones who have both fallen asleep in their highchairs, faces pink and sticky with semi-dried ice cream. I smile at the sight. That is goddamn cute.

"Freddie and Margot are going to bed too, Lucas." Rhiannon smiles. "We can play games tomorrow though, okay?"

"Oh, I don't know," I say, shaking my head. "Is that in the schedule, Lis?"

"Shut up, Partridge."

Oscar gasps, "Mummy!"

"Mummy pays half the mortgage, she's allowed to say that," Lisa states, matter-of-factly.

"I was thinking I should probably head over to the hotel and get settled." Nel says quietly. "I can call a taxi and help you clear up while I wait for it, then I'll just catch up with you tomorrow."

"No taxi required," I smile at her across the table. "I'll drive you."

"Oh, that's really not necessary," she says, avoiding eye contact.

"Well, it seems a bit silly for you to get a taxi when I'm driving to the hotel anyway."

"You are?"

"Sure, I'm staying there too."

That dear in headlights look is back. She goes a little pale, and her eyes are wide. "Oh."

CHAPTER FIVE
"What do you think Nelly-Belly means?"

NEL

J ake drives us to the hotel in silence. Then he helps me with my bags, wheeling my suitcase behind him as he carries his duffle over one shoulder. I feel like I should explain why I have such a large case. I was going to make use of the hotel, which according to the website has nice boutique-y rooms that would make for great recording backdrops. In my giant suitcase, I have a lot of makeup as I thought I'd film some tutorials for TikTok and YouTube. There are also several rather beautiful lingerie sets in there for some posing tutorials, although they don't take up that much room.

Before I think of my excuses, we're walking through the double doors of reception. There's tinny Christmas music playing overhead and a young girl sat behind a slightly beat up looking desk. She smiles brightly as we approach, her eyes blatantly roaming over Jake.

"Good evening, welcome to Orchard Inn."

"Thank you," Jake smiles. "We have two reservations for the next few days. Jake Partridge and Penelope Forrest."

I stand awkwardly behind Jake's shoulder, feeling ridiculously jealous that the sweet blonde behind the counter is on the receiving end of one of Jake Partridge's signature smiles.

"I have your reservation here Mr. Partridge, you're in room 208, here's your key." She slides a key across the counter. He takes it, stepping aside for me to come forward. She looks at me with a smile that doesn't reach her eyes, waiting expectantly for me to say something. "Can I help with anything else?"

"Err…my room key please?" I mumble.

"You need an extra key for the room? We can offer one at an extra charge."

"I need my own room," I say with a little more snap than I usually have.

"Oh…" she looks at her computer again. "We only have one reservation here for Mr. Jake Partridge and Miss. Penelope Forrest."

Panic. My heart is pounding.

"That should be two separate bookings," Jake says, coming back to stand by my side.

She shakes her head, chewing on her bottom lip. "We have one booking for one room but given two guest names. Partridge and Forrest."

I lean my elbows on the counter and hold my head in my hands. This is a nightmare.

"Does the room, by any chance, have two beds?" Jake asks, his voice far calmer than I feel.

"No sir, it's a king room with one bed." She looks at him apologetically but seems confused by my obvious distress.

"Do you have any other rooms available?" I ask, standing straight and sniffing in a calming breath.

"I'm sorry ma'am but, we're fully booked for Christmas."

"There is nothing?"

She shakes her head, her look pitying. I can't help the groan that leaves me. Jake checks his watch and sighs.

"I can drive home, Nel. I only live an hour away."

I look over at him, he looks tired. We stayed later than planned helping Lisa tidy up despite her protests while Harry entertained the family in the lounge. He's only had one glass of wine with dinner, but I can't say I'd be too happy with him driving in the dark for an hour on icy roads.

"It's fine," I say, resigned. "I mean, if you want to leave, sure, go ahead. But you must be tired, and you've been drinking."

"I drove us here," he argues with a smile.

"Still, I'd rather you didn't drive more than necessary. We can get through tonight and we'll sort something out tomorrow."

He nods, grabbing the handle of my case once again and waiting expectantly for me to follow, which of course, I do. The room is nice—really nice. Exactly what I'd wanted for my planned posts, but I definitely won't get a chance to do them while Jake is here. The plush king-sized bed crowded with cushions of varying jewel tones in satins and velvets stands proudly in the centre of the room. Like a taunting devil, smirking at me. *Eurgh*. I scan the room carefully, twice for good measure, and see there is not a sofa or chaise lounge in sight. The bed is the only option for sleeping. I can feel anxiety roiling in my belly, mixing with the cocktail and wine.

"Festive," Jake says with a smile, jerking his chin toward the small desk where a fibre optic tree sits.

I'm not feeling festive, I'm feeling exhausted. I had a busy morning in the studio followed by travelling on the crowded train three days before Christmas and I'm just about ready to collapse. Jake drops his duffle on one side of the bed and wheels my case to the other. I guess we have sides of the bed now. Why does that make the knot in my stomach bunch tighter?

In silence, because I'm not sure I have any small talk left in me, I head to my side of the bed, take my coat and hat off, placing them on the small armchair. I kneel on the soft black carpet and unzip my case, lifting the lid and quickly snapping it shut again as I realise what's on top. The several sets of new lingerie I was sent from my sponsor, Soft Curves, lay on top of everything I need to get ready for bed. I glance up at Jake and he's staring at my closed case. He saw. I'm in literal Hell.

30

"I, uh…I'll go use the bathroom," he says backing into the closed door, before turning round and opening it to slip through quickly.

I hurriedly rearrange my case, shoving handfuls of lace and silk to the bottom and bringing my bathroom stuff to the top. I groan when I realise the pyjamas I brought are a matching set of tiny shorts that let half my substantial arse hang out, and a strappy tank top in green satin with cute little mistletoe sprigs all over. It was another gift that I'd modelled for Soft Curves back in November to help them launch their Christmas line and I thought it would be cute to bring them for Christmas. Of course, when I'd made that decision, I hadn't counted on sharing a bed with Jake Partridge. I don't know what would be worse; Jake seeing me in this barely-there ensemble, or my usual ratty t-shirt and Garfield pyjama bottoms that I normally sleep in.

With Jake in the bathroom, I take a few breaths before starting my usual night-time skincare, taking comfort in the methodical routine. Makeup removed, I massage in my night cream, dot eye cream around my eyes, and use the cool facial roller on my cheeks and forehead.

"What is that?" I jump at Jake's voice; I didn't even hear him coming out of the bathroom.

"It's a jade Derma-Roller." When he just blinks at me, I can feel the slight pull of a smile and I continue. "It's supposed to boost collagen and give you a good glow and reduce puffiness."

"Does it work?" He raises a quizzical brow.

"No clue but I saw it on TikTok and I'm a sucker for an advert," I say with a shrug.

He huffs out a laugh, that sexy as Hell smile on his beautiful face making my insides bubble. "Well you look glowy and unpuffy to me, so I guess it works." He winks at me and my mouth dries. "Bathroom's yours Forrest."

I grab my pyjamas and toiletry bag and head into the bathroom. His things are lined up on one side of the sink leaving the other side for me. I look at the closed door for a brief second before picking up his aftershave and giving it a sniff. That spice and orangey citrus smell fills my nostrils and I see Jake through closed eyes. What the Hell does Jake wear to bed? Will he be shirtless? Because, honestly, I think I might have an aneurism.

I undress and look at myself in the mirror. I have worked hard on accepting myself, on loving myself, and embracing the body I live in. Eighty percent of the time, I do just fine. But looking at my reflection right now, I don't see Nel Forrest, I see Nelly-Belly. My tummy is soft and jiggles when I move. Without the makeup, there's nothing contouring my face into acceptable angles; instead it's round and I have a double chin. Harry's joke when I declined ice-cream runs through my head with everyone chuckling because of course it's funny that the only fat person in attendance wouldn't want dessert. I wanted it, but I had this image of everyone staring at me while I ate, judging me, and I couldn't bear it.

I put my satin pjs on and examine myself closely. My arms are too big and my legs have dimples that most would call cellulite. I don't keep up with my fake tan in the winter, so I'm pale too. Without the support of my favourite bra, my large breasts hang a little lower than I'd like and I'm worried that I may wake up with one trying to make a hasty escape from my top. That would just be the cherry on top of the Christmas pudding; Jake Partridge waking up with my unrestrained tit in his face. Not that his face would be anywhere near my tits. *Right?*

With a deep breath, I open the door and find Jake stood right in front of me in plaid pyjama bottoms and *no shirt*. I must lose all the colour in my face.

"You okay, Nelly-Belly?"

I snap. "Can you *not* call me that?" My fists clench at my sides as I stand in the doorway to the bathroom, my satin short shorts and camisole feeling far too exposing.

"I, uh. I'm sorry." He seems so confused and concerned that some of my temper dies, but tears sting at the back of my eyes as the evening weighs me down.

"It's fine," I sigh. "I'm just tired." I crawl into the bed and lie on my side, giving Jake my back, hugging the edge of the mattress to keep as much distance between us as possible. The bed dips as he presumably gets in too. I switch off the light to try and get some sleep, but I can feel the tension bunching up my muscles from the evening gone, and from the fact that I'm in bed with Jake Freakin' Partridge. The light from the fibre optic tree that neither of us bothered turning off still sets an ambient glow across the room changing from pink to purple to blue.

"Is it because I'm not family?" Jake asks gently.

I turn to him, screwing up my face in confusion. "What?"

"Is it just meant to be a family nickname or something?" He's lying on his back and turns his head on the pillow so we're eye to eye. "I didn't mean to upset you, I thought everyone called you that. If it's just a family thing, I'm sorry I overstepped."

"Jake," I huff, letting frustration get the better of me. "I don't like *anyone* calling me fat, don't take it personally."

"What?" He jerks back, outraged. "I didn't call you fat!"

"What do you think Nelly-Belly means?" I whisper hiss to avoid screeching like an errant child.

"It's just a cute nickname. It doesn't mean *that*." His confidence in his own words seems to dwindle throughout his statement. If I wasn't dying for this conversation to just be over, I'd find his furrowed brow and the way his eyes dart about as though he's trying to figure out a puzzle very cute.

"It's the nickname Harry gave me when I was twelve years old and I dared to wear a bikini for the first time on holiday. He kept following me around, poking my stomach, and shouting Nelly-Belly. Then he kept it up at home where you and all his little rugby mates caught on and started calling me Nelly-Belly. Then everyone at school got the memo. One guy from my year went to the same university as me and although I was thankful to have someone I knew around, he called me Nelly-Belly on a night out and everyone thought it was cute and funny, so at university I was Nelly-Belly for the three years until I graduated.

I should be thankful really, I mean Nelly-Belly was one of the better ones. Beats Nelly the Elephant, Penelope Pig, or the old classic, Fatty."

Jake looks disgusted. I probably shouldn't be bringing his attention to my jiggly stomach when he has to share a bed with me, I don't want to gross him out. Still, I wrap up my speech.

"So, yeah. Any of our mutual acquaintances probably know me as Nelly-Belly but I have spent long enough with my own friends who just know me as Nel now that it's jarring to come back to Nelly-Belly. I was prepared for it when we were at Harry's, but I was expecting to be coming back to my own hotel room where I could be Nel again. And honestly, I need the break. So please, just while we're here, don't call me that." I think I'm keeping the pain out of my eyes, hoping he can't see any tears and that my voice is strong enough.

It's hard to remain neutral when today has been one blow after the other. First, I had to start celebrations for my first Christmas without my parents. Then I was reintroduced to my brother's teasing in a crowd of people I hardly know, which was only worsened by the fact that my childhood crush was there and will be here for the whole frigging holiday. On top of that, I have to share a hotel room with said crush when all I wanted to do at the end of the day is decompress in my own company. And the cherry on top of the nightmare sundae? I have now had to explain to that crush how the cutesy little nickname he's been calling me for sixteen years actually hurts my feelings, because I'm fat. A fact he probably doesn't need brought to his attention.

God, I wish I was at my Mum and Dad's house right now, lying in my childhood bed, staring up at the Chris Hemsworth poster on my ceiling. I wish I could hear them downstairs bickering about how loud the TV is, Mum telling Dad to turn it down or they'd keep me up. I wish I was full of Mum's steak and ale pie that she always made, and Dad's festive mash potatoes, which were just made with double cream instead of milk. Because Mum and Dad were firm believers that Christmas meant doubling calories for the pure Hell of it. I wish I was safe in assuming that Dad would poke his head in my bedroom door before he came to bed to 'check on me' even though I'm a grown woman and hear him whisper 'love you Nels' before pulling my door closed. And just like that, a tear slips free and trails over my temple.

Jake looks at me with a pained expression. Is that pity? "Nel…"

"Night, Jake." I turn over again so he can't see my face and I concentrate on keeping my breathing even and quiet so he can't hear me cry.

There's a minute of silence before he sighs and I feel the bed move as he turns over. "Goodnight, Nel."

CHAPTER SIX
"I am *not* your brother."

NEL

I'm hot. Okay, this is beyond hot, I'm *sweltering*. The blankets have become a furnace in the night, and I try to kick them off only to find my legs pinned. I panic for a second thinking I have somehow woken up without the use of my extremities until realisation slowly rises like the dawn outside. I'm not wrapped in the blankets; I'm being hugged like a koala by Jake. My face is right in the centre of his chest, both his arms holding me there as his chin rests on the top of my head, one of his legs is over my hip, the other between my knees. *How the Hell did we get into this position?* I'm a heavy sleeper and don't normally move much in the night, but I distinctly remember falling asleep with a good two feet of mattress between us.

I try to wriggle free so I can get to the bathroom when something twitches against my hip. *Oh shit.* Jake Partridge has morning wood, and I just rubbed up against it. He groans in his sleep, his fingers flexing against my back as he moves his face down to bury in my hair. When one hand slowly strokes down my back and doesn't stop until he has a handful of my arse and squeezes, my eyes practically bulge out of their sockets.

"Uh…Jake?"

He mutters incoherently.

"Jake you're kind of groping me a little bit." I wriggle against him again, trying to free myself from his vice like grip and this time his moan is overtly sexual.

His eyes flick open and those beautiful irises stare at me, both of us still and silent for a moment. He blinks a few times as he comes round and puts together the scene. "Sorry," he mumbles.

"That's okay." I swallow. "You can...uh...you can take your hand off my butt now."

He retracts his hand as if I'd burned him and rolls to his back, untangling us so I'm free to crawl out of bed and into the bathroom, grabbing what I need from my case on the way.

I shower and wash my hair, twisting it into a thick braid so it dries into waves before I work on my makeup. I can still feel where Jake's hand was on my behind and the feel of his hard-on against my front. That's just nature, Nel. It has nothing to do with you, *calm the Hell down*. Once I'm happy with my eyeliner and have applied my new 'Festive Berry' lipstick that I treated myself to while doing Christmas shopping, I head back into the room. I try to avoid eye contact so Jake can't see the blush in my cheeks, and it's easier than you might think because his eyes are the last thing on my mind. Jake has removed his pyjamas in preparation for his shower and is stood checking his phone in nothing but a pair of light grey boxers. He's all thick thighs, bulging biceps, and amazing abs. Teachers are not meant to look that good.

"It's uh, it's all yours," I say, trying to find something interesting on the carpet to focus on.

"Thanks," his voice is rough from sleep. He rolls his towel and heads towards me, to the bathroom. "Oh, and Nel?"

"Yeah?" I still don't look in his eye as I wait for him to apologise for groping me.

"Don't feel bad for staring." Uh...*what?* "I kind of like it when you look at me like that." He winks at me again. Holy shit, that does funny things to my nether regions. And he likes it when I...I wasn't...*what?*

He chuckles as he passes by—my mouth agape—and closes the bathroom door with a click. I don't know what just happened, so I shake it off and get dressed into something other than my ridiculous pyjamas. Deciding on jeans and an oversized crisp white shirt, I spend a minute or two perfecting the French tuck and arranging everything to look just so. I'm pleased with my outfit; a black leather belt with a nice silver buckle to match my silver hooped earrings and my black leather boots with silver studding. I throw on a long grey cardigan to keep warm just as Jake comes out of the bathroom, the smell of soap and that delicious aftershave travelling into the bedroom with the steam from his shower. He's all ready to go, the same jeans as yesterday with a tight black t-shirt that stretches over his biceps and does nothing to conceal the expanse of muscle on his torso. Stopping in the doorway briefly, he blinks at me a couple of times.

"You, uh, you look nice." He seems surprised by his own words, and I can feel my blush.

"Thanks."

"Ready to go? We have an itinerary to keep to."

I snort. Actually snort like a pig. Covering my nose with my hand, I try to hide it even though it's already out in the world. Jake's amused smirk has me fighting my own smile. "Shut up."

"Didn't say a thing."

Frost had settled on every available surface overnight, making everything white as though it had snowed. Delicate icicles hang from barren branches and the pavement seems to shimmer in the early morning sun. We could walk to Harry and Lisa's from the hotel as it's on the same road. Pear Street and the surrounding roads were all once part of a huge orchard, many years ago. When the area was developed, a new suburb in Surrey was created and a huge number of the plots were sold to self-builders, so all the houses are unique and beautiful in their own way. Pear Street runs through the middle of the area and holds some of the most expensive and extravagant houses, which then thinned out to make way for several small independent shops and restaurants with the hotel at the end of it all. A twenty-minute walk through the cute parade and we would be at Harry's. But

Jake takes one look at the small heel on my boots and says we'll drive.

"I am perfectly comfortable in these," I say, climbing into the passenger seat of his Volkswagen Atlas. "I could walk."

"That's good, have you seen the itinerary for today?" he asks, blasting the heater to defrost the windscreen.

I pull the schedule from my old faithful Michael Kors handbag that my parents had bought me a few years ago, and check today's events.

09:30-11:00 – Breakfast at Pear Street.

11:15-13:00 – Walk along the common.

"Great," I sigh. "A nice long walk in the cold."

"You want to go change your boots?" he smirks.

"No," I answer stubbornly. I mean, these boots *are* comfortable and it's only a two-inch heel. Plus the common is a network of paved walkways going around the hilly green so the ground will be even. But, if I'm being completely honest with myself, trainers would probably be a safer option.

"Okay," he says but he sounds unconvinced as we pull out of our parking spot. "Hey, about earlier—"

"I wasn't staring!" I blurt out.

"Oh, Nels," he chuckles. "You were totally staring." He turns to face me to give me one of those powerhouse smiles before turning back to the road. "But that's not what I'm talking about. I mean this morning, when we woke up." He clears his throat looking a lot less confident. "I'm sorry for uh, you know."

"Grabbing my arse?" I ask innocently, enjoying his discomfort a little too much.

"Yeah, that. I'm a bit of a cuddly sleeper and I guess in my comatose state, my body didn't really understand the dynamics at play. It was inappropriate and I apologise."

Oh. It's inappropriate. Of course, it is. I'm his best-friend's annoying little sister, and he's a god among men, working with children every day, and volunteering to fight fires in his down time. I'm the overweight social caterpillar who'd rather cocoon herself than deal with people, and who's made a career by basically taking her clothes off for the camera. But hearing the words from his mouth stings. It really stings.

"It's fine," I say quietly.

"No," he shakes his head. "It's not."

"Well, if it's any consolation, I think my comatose body didn't understand the assignment either. I don't know how I ended up in the middle of the bed."

"Not a cuddly sleeper?" he asks with a cheeky smile.

Oh God, why are my cheeks heating again. "Actually, uh, I have never slept with anyone before."

"What?" He snaps his head toward me, swerving the car nearly into the kerb.

"I mean physically *slept* with someone, I'm not a virgin or anything," I ramble. He stares ahead with a strange expression on his face. "Don't know why I felt the need to tell you that."

"How have you never slept in the same bed as someone?"

I shrug, looking out the window. "I like my space; I don't like to share."

"You were sharing quite well this morning," he states while side eyeing me.

"Mmm."

There are a few beats of silence in which I start feeling more uncomfortable and wanting to explain myself. "And I have had a boyfriend. I don't know why Harry is so sure I haven't."

He nods thoughtfully. "Did you ever tell Harry about a boyfriend?"

"No," I snort. "He doesn't want to hear about my love life."

"Maybe that's why he was unsure you've ever had a relationship. How is he supposed to know if you don't tell him?"

It's too early and I am not caffeinated enough for logic, so I just stare at him.

"Okay, so tell me about the boyfriend." He stares out the windscreen with a narrowed brow.

"Not much to tell. He was okay. Made his own cheese. Bit weird."

"How did you avoid sharing a bed with him?"

"You're getting very personal for nine o'clock in the morning." I glare at him.

"We were a lot more personal at seven o'clock this morning."

I roll my eyes. "I usually told him I had to work early or that I wasn't feeling great. To be honest he wasn't all that bothered."

"Idiot."

"Excuse me?"

"He's an idiot. If I was with you, I'd definitely be bothered about not getting to share your bed."

My eyes widen. "You mean any girl?"

It's his turn to shrug. "Sure."

"Well, I need my sleep and I would have thought I'd struggle to relax with another person in bed with me. Until last night, that is."

He nods. "So, what happened then? With the boyfriend."

I sigh, I don't want to tell him. I don't want him to think of all the reasons I'm not a suitable girlfriend even though he would never think of me that way. "He didn't like some of the posts I put online."

"The more risqué pictures, I'm guessing?"

I swallow hard, the skin at the back of my neck prickling. "You've seen them?"

His lip twitch before he schools his features. "A few."

Oh God. Jake Partridge has seen me in my underwear. And he groped my butt in his sleep. Life is a crazy thing. "Right. Well, he didn't like them and decided he didn't want to continue our relationship." When he says nothing, I feel like I need to keep talking. "I know some people might think it's not appropriate,

41

but I happen to like what I do so it's really none of their business. You boys are all welcome to your opinions, and I know Harry thinks I'm one partner away from making porn—"

"Let's be clear," Jake raises his voice slightly to cut me off. "I am *not* your brother."

Er, okay. What am I meant to say to that? "Good, else that arse groping would have been *really* inappropriate."

He grins so wide it looks salacious, and I can't help but stare at his lips stretched over perfect, white teeth. "All I'm saying is, don't assume I feel the same as H. I think it's really cool what you do."

"Thanks," I whisper over a harsh exhale.

We've pulled up at the house and Jake gets out without another word. I take half a second to put my game face on, then follow him. But he doesn't go to the front door; he rounds the hood to hold my door open. Once I'm safely out, he closes the car door and crowds me against it. Earth and time stand still and all I can hear is the roaring of blood in my ears as he leans closer to me. My gaze drops to those lips again, focussing on the way his dark beard frames them. I want so badly to run my fingers through it, to feel how coarse or soft it is, to feel the sharpness of his jawline beneath it. My tongue darts out to wet my parted lips and his eyes flick to track the movement.

What is happening?

"Just so you know," he speaks low and soft. "I've seen all of your posts, Nel. Every. Last. One. At first, I wanted to be supportive by following you. But then… then I couldn't stop if I tried."

He pushes off the car and strolls to the front door without looking back. Leaving me reeling, opening and closing my mouth like a freakin' guppy still trying to figure out what any of that even means.

CHAPTER SEVEN
"Avenge me."

JAKE

Breakfast is a friggin' spread. Lisa is always amazing at hosting even when I pop by for a beer on a weekend, she has snacks at the ready. But this is something else. Eggs, bacon, sausage, hashbrowns, fried bread, toast, croissants, homemade jam, waffles, syrup, pancakes, and I think there were some chocolate pastries, but my Godsons have disappeared under the table with plates piled high with them. Everyone is tucking in with what can only be described as gusto and telling Lisa how amazing she is. She waves her hand at the compliments dismissively. But Harry doesn't let her, telling her how incredible everything is and placing gentle kisses first on her head and then her protruding baby bump.

"Hey, Nelly-Belly," Harry calls down the table.

She freezes with a hash brown halfway to her plate looking at her brother, waiting for him to continue.

"Try and save some for everyone else, yeah?" He chuckles to himself and goes back to speaking to Charles. Nel's eyes dart around the table before she puts what I believe is her first hash brown back. She sits back with just some eggs and bacon on her plate and eats slowly and self-consciously. I suddenly want to punch my best friend, which is a completely new feeling. Has he always been such a dick? I fear he may have been and I have failed to ever notice. I love Harry, he's like a brother to me, but perhaps the teasing banter we enjoy as friends doesn't quite translate to siblinghood. Has Nel always been affected by words?

How much have I unwittingly contributed to whatever it is that has her retreating back into her shell and moving further from the siren I have been dying to meet?

Because I'm a little pissed at Harry, and because I'm trying to remind Nel of who she is, I clear my throat until everyone is looking. "Nel, have you ever photographed any celebrities?"

I know she has. Her popularity on social media has drawn the attention of some very minor celebrities and they have done some of the more risqué shoots, probably to boost their own online interaction. But if Lisa's cousin hears anything about a celebrity, she'll immediately want to see photographic evidence. Nel stares at me across the table, knowing now that I'm fully aware of her content, she clearly understands that I'm bringing it up on purpose. And she doesn't seem happy about it. I just smile innocently at her as everyone waits eagerly for a reply.

"I, um…well—"

"Oh my God! You have, haven't you?" Rhiannon's eyes are wide and excited.

"Well, *'celebrity'* may be a bit of a strong word."

"We'll be the judge of that," Hen says, matching her daughter's energy.

"Uh, okay…" Nel seems to think for a second and I dart a look at Harry who is fidgeting uncomfortably. Honestly, he's not normally such a stick in the mud. But Lisa's dad being an actual Lord and the founder and previous CEO of a highly successful tech company, and her mother being an ex-minister, he does get understandably flustered in their presence. "Do you know Kaci Kai?"

Rhiannon and Hen share an excited glance. "You mean the woman from Mayfair MILFs?"

I snort at Harry's grimace. He told me Lisa was an avid watcher of the reality TV show in question and after we suffered through a couple of episodes with her, we agreed that neither of us would like to F any of the Ms. Not a looks thing. More an unbelievably-annoying-whiny-first-world-problems-toxic-drama personality thing.

"Oh my God, I love that show," Lisa groans.

"Yeah. Well, I photographed her." Nel nods, looking down at the table.

"Ooh, let me see!" Rhiannon stretches an arm out as though Nel should just pass her phone over.

Nel sighs and looks at all the children. "They're not exactly suitable for present company."

"Oh," Rhiannon says, confused and then as realisation dawns, "Oooohh." She smirks at Nel. "Yeah, after the discussion last night, I looked you up on Instagram. You're a bit of a dark horse, aren't you?"

"Oh?" Charles asks.

"Right," Harry stands. "Everyone appears to be finished, let's get cleared up and head out for that walk, wouldn't want to overrun the schedule, would we, dearest?" He looks at Lisa for support and she rolls her eyes at his neurosis.

"No, darling." She stands to collect some dishes and glares at me, circling a clenched fist in a stirring motion, mouthing '*shit stirrer.*' I give her my best, most charming smile and wink. She just smirks, shaking her head as she walks away. I look over to Nel to see that she's watching the exchange and I catch something in her eyes that flares heat through the lower half of my body. *Was that jealousy, Penelope?*

We drive to Orchard Common as Lisa pulls the pregnancy card and says she's too round to walk to a walk. The grounds are high and hilly and there is a light dusting of snow on the grassy areas. The boys immediately start throwing snowballs at each other and the little ones are desperate to join, toddling precariously on uneven ground. Luke stays close to them, helping them ball tiny fistfuls of snow to throw at Lucas and

45

Oscar who return fire with such gentleness, I feel immensely proud of them.

"Uncle Jake," Lucas calls. "Come play with us."

Well, I can't turn down a good snowball fight, so that's what we do. All while the '*grown-ups*' walk along the paved pathway, talking about boring '*grown-up*' things. We follow them while sticking to the grass, trying to hit each other with snow, although our ammunition is sparce. We soon come across a playground and the kids quickly lose sight of our game. Undeterred by the wet snow on all the equipment, they're soon scrambling on climbing frames and slides while Rhiannon and Luke each help a twin into a baby swing. The grandparents head into the playground too, doting on grandchildren and indulging them in fun and enthusiastic play.

"Hey, Oscar," Harry calls as I'm approaching him, Lisa, and Nel to wait with them on the sidelines.

Oscar, who has climbed to the top of the climbing frame and is just poised to descend the tube slide, looks up at his father. "Yeah?"

"Be careful in there, don't get stuck like Aunty Nelly-Belly did," Harry chuckles like he's just made a hilarious joke.

Nel rolls her eyes and then calls, but quieter than Harry's bolshy voice. "The slide was old and cracked and my coat got caught."

Oscar looks down the winding tunnel dubiously and I take pity on him. "You're alright, bud." I call over. "I inspected it, no cracks."

He relaxes and gives me a goofy smile before flinging himself down the slide and emerging from the other end, giggling. I start back over to where my friends are standing on the sidelines and although I'm a few feet away, I still hear Harry's teasing.

"Still sticking with the coat story, Nels? Sure you just didn't fit?" He tickles her side and she squirms away. I'm vaguely aware that Lisa makes a disapproving noise at her husband, but I want to shake him up a bit. I swoop down to scoop up a handful of snow and throw it right at his chest.

Then everything happens in slow motion. Harry bends to tie his shoe as Nel turns to look at me and my snowball hits her square in the face. Her eyes scrunch closed as her mouth falls open in shock. Taking a step back from the impact, her heel must find some ice and she goes down like a cartoon character who's just stood on a banana skin. Arms circling at her sides like propellers and her legs scissoring in the air until she lands with a thud on her back.

Oh shit.

Running over, I practically shove Harry out the way before he has a chance to get to her side. Lisa is bent double to look at her prone sister-in-law but doesn't crouch, for obvious reasons. I drop to my knees and take Nel's face in my hands, wiping melted snow from under her eyes with my thumbs.

"God, Nel. I'm so sorry. Are you okay?"

She slowly blinks her eyes open and looks at me. Those beautiful browns glass over, and my chest constricts, *please don't cry*. The pain in her eyes has me on the brink of tears myself.

"How could you?" she rasps.

A little taken back by her reaction, I stutter slightly. "I…I'm sorry, Nel. I was aiming for Harry."

She widens her eyes as though that would have been worse. "Brother," she calls with a pained wail.

Harry falls to his knees on the other side. "I'm here, little sister," he says, crying.

Okay, *what*?

"I…I won't make it," she gasps and then coughs.

Oh no.

"Don't leave me, Nels. I can't do this without you." Harry takes his sister's hand in his and lets out an Academy Award worthy cry into the sky.

I slowly stand and start backing away. I know this game, and I always lose.

"Avenge me," Nelly whispers before her head slumps to the side with her tongue hanging out, dead eyes staring at me, but I don't miss the small spark of life that says *run*.

Harry rises and pins me with a glare, one I know all too well from our boyhood games. See, there was a time when we were much *much* younger and Nel wasn't so awkward around me, when she was desperate to play with her big brother and his friends. The thing is, we played rough and we didn't want little Penelope to get hurt. So while Harry and I were cops and robbers, Nel would play Harry's accomplice who'd get eliminated early in the game. Caught in the crossfire. Then Harry would avenge her death by coming at me. I built up a muscular physique after Harry and I joined the rugby team at school, but Harry has always been a bit of a bulldozer and was always able to pin me easily.

By now, everyone has crowded around Nel's 'body,' most of them completely confused as to what is happening.

"Forrests!" Harry bellows, like Captain America summoning his Avengers. "Attack!"

I run. I can hear the boys' war cries behind me as they try to catch up, they never will unless I let them. But it's not them I'm worried about. I get a fair distance away before Harry executes a perfect tackle and I hit the ground with enough force to knock the wind out of me.

"Fuck," he pants. "It's been a while since we've done that." He lays next to me on the cold, wet grass.

"You haven't pinned me for three seconds yet, I could still get away," I say, but my huffing breath betrays me.

My best friend laughs with more relaxed joy than I've seen from him since the festivities began. "Yeah, but we're both too old to keep going."

"Speak for yourself," I scoff, but I can't help my smile.

"Plus, you'd really disappoint them if you start running again."

"Huh?"

On cue, Lucas and Oscar dog-pile on top of me. I grunt and groan in protest. Of course, I could roll away from them quite easily, but I admit defeat and surrender, much to their utter delight. The rest of our group make their way over to us, all smiles and mirth at our antics. I lock eyes with Nel, and my body sags in relief to see her smiling although Lisa is examining the back of her coat with concern.

"Are you sure you're okay?" Lisa asks. "You came down pretty hard."

Nel looks away from me with that signature blush. "Oh, I'm fine."

"I really am sorry, Nel," I say as I stand, depositing the boys on the ground.

She gives me a bright and unhindered smile. "That's okay, I'm sure you'll make it up to me." Walking away without a second look, I'm left wondering if Nel Forrest was flirting with me.

Fuck, I hope so.

CHAPTER EIGHT:
"Who's shit stirring now, woman?"

NEL

O kay, I think I've bruised my back. But it's fine. I actually found the look of abject horror on Jake's face when he'd rushed to my side was ever so slightly satisfying. Jake was worried about me. And this morning, he woke up with a— might I say, massive?—hard-on while wrapped around me, then he caged me against his car like Dermot Mulroney did to Debra Messing in The Wedding Date. *God, I love that movie.* Now, I'll get a lady-boner every time I watch that scene.

He apologises at least a dozen more times as we drive back to the house on Pear Street, and at least a dozen times I tell him it's okay. Approaching the house, I note the temporary yellow signs along the road and that some of the roads have been cordoned off. We step into the house just after everyone else, grateful for the relief from my heels as I remove my boots—not that I would be admitting that to Jake—and take off my favourite camel coat. There is a huge wet patch on the back and some mud that I'm really hoping will come off.

"I'll pay for the dry-cleaning," Jake mutters as though he read my mind.

I snort at him; I've never seen him so humble. We're crowded in the porch, both of us in the doorway, and I look at him with a soft smile. "Get over it, Jake. I'm fine."

He takes a half step forward so we're too close for social norms. "I don't ever want to hurt you, Nel." The weight of his words suggests that he is talking about more than just a light bruising. The smell of spice and orange wraps around me in a warmth that seeps into my bones and seems to soothe any tension that was there.

Any response I have to his statement is washed away by the sound of an amused '*ooooohhhh*' from the hallway. Snapping my head to follow the sound, I see Lisa stood in the hall with a very amused smirk on her face. "Are you two going to kiss?"

"What?! No!" I nearly shriek, horrified that Jake might be disgusted at the thought.

"Then whatcha doing lurking under the mistletoe?" She grins like the Cheshire Cat.

As if in slow motion, both Jake and I look up to see a perfectly formed sprig of fresh mistletoe, tied with red ribbon. We stare for a minute.

Jake turns to Lisa with suspicious eyes and points to the offending foliage. "Was this here yesterday?"

She shrugs. "No, I was up early and thought I'd dot a few around the house, keep everyone on their toes." Leaning against the wall and resting her hands on her giant belly, she raises her eyebrows expectantly. "Well go on, you wouldn't want to have seven years of bad luck for ignoring tradition."

I scrunch my face up. "I'm pretty sure that's just for breaking a mirror."

"Still, probably wouldn't chance it," she says with a seriousness I can only assume is faked.

Jake narrows his eyes at her further but he's struggling to keep the smile from his face. "Who's shit stirring now, woman?"

She pushes off the wall with a laugh and walks away but throws a wink over her shoulder. When Jake faces me again, I panic. I'm not the type of girl Jake Partridge kisses in porchways.

"We should join the others," I mumble, slipping away and heading down the hall without a second glance.

Everyone is gathered in the large living room, and for the first time, I can really appreciate the opulence of Lisa's beautiful decorations. Green garlands adorned with plush, red, velvet ribbons. Everything is meticulously placed and each decoration unique and artisanal. No cheap multi-packs of baubles here.

The kids are all sat on the floor, the boys are playing with the twins, crawling about and making a lot of noise. Charles and Cami are cosied up on one sofa, his arm lovingly draped over her shoulders and Gordan and Hen are on the other. Each couple has a seat free next to them and Lisa and Harry are perched on dining chairs that have been brought in from the kitchen. Rhiannon and Luke had disappeared upstairs for a quick nap, making the most of the free babysitting. I would have assumed that was some sort of cover for going up to bone, but after seeing the dark circles under their eyes, I know that it was no ruse.

"Have a seat, duck," Charles says, pointing to the seat cushion next to his wife.

"Yes, Nel." Cami smiles at me so genuinely, I can't help but offer one back. "Please sit down, let us get to know each other, we're family after all."

The idea of them 'getting to know me' is a little terrifying, I don't want to embarrass myself or Harry. I know he's funny about my job and his in-laws finding out the true nature of my photography.

"Rhiannon showed me some of your photographs from your website," Camilla says and my heart stops for a second. "They're absolutely stunning; you're incredibly talented."

I blink at her.

"Yes, very beautiful." Charles nods and looks at me with something akin to pride. "You have your own studio space?"

"Uh, yes. I mean I rent, I don't own it or anything."

"Still, renting your own commercial space in London is impressive. You must be proud of yourself."

"I…" I take a moment, a more genuine smile stretching at my face. "I am."

Charles smiles back at me beneath his whiting blonde moustache, his eyes crinkling with the force of it. "I'm sure your parents were incredibly proud too. I would be."

That whooshes the air from my lungs and my eyes sting with unshed tears. Cami notices and instead of giving me the expected 'I'm sorry your parents are dead' speech, she closes her hand over mine on my leg and offers me a reassuring squeeze that seems to say it for her. I'm grateful not to have to hear the words. I'm also grateful to hear that my parents would be proud of me. They told me, of course, but my career hadn't taken off until after Dad got sick so there were always other things that we talked about. The conversations over the last couple of years were usually a lot more sombre.

"Thank you," I whisper as a single tear escapes.

Charles reaches over Cami's shoulders to pat mine while Cami squeezes my hand again. From there, the conversation becomes lighter as we talk about their trip to Mexico this summer, and they ask if I travel much. *Not as much as I'd like*. I find them easy to talk to and despite Harry's obvious concerns, they aren't offended by my work in the slightest.

My eyes keep drifting to Jake on the opposite sofa, talking to Hen, Gordan, Lisa, and Harry as well as engaging with the kids. He has little Margot on his knee, bouncing her until she giggles, and he brings Lucas and Oscar into the conversation with the grown-ups. Although Oscar is young enough to be snuggled on his dad's lap, he still answers thoughtfully every time Jake asks his thoughts on their conversation. Lucas sits on the floor at Jake's feet, facing and mimicking him by bouncing baby Freddie on his leg. Both boys look at Jake with such adoration and love that I get a weird pang of guilt.

I hardly see the boys. I hardly see Harry. The last time I spent any time with my brother was at the probate meeting to discuss our parents' assets with the solicitors. It was a difficult meeting and Harry had asked if I wanted to go to lunch after, but I was too drained. I just wanted to get home, get to bed, and cry. He'd been disappointed, not able to hide the rolling of his eyes and I'd felt guilty. But not enough to go to lunch with him.

I've been invited to Harry and Lisa's many times over the years: BBQs, kids' birthday parties, a Halloween party. But I've never come, claiming work was keeping me too busy. I only really saw them when we all got together with Mum and Dad because I felt comfortable with that dynamic of having Mum and Dad as a buffer between Harry and me.

I can't remember exactly when he started poking fun and using me as the butt of every joke he made to his friends. I know he didn't do it to hurt me; he did it to impress them. I used to try and laugh along, so he probably thought I was enjoying his hilarity as much as everyone else. He'd tease me for being chubby, for being bad at sports, for being clumsy and awkward, for anything really. It was always done as a joke and never to be cruel. When we were both a little older, he seemed to have such large opinions about my life, who I spent my time with, what I wanted to do with my life, deciding to rent in the city instead of trying to buy a place of my own. I love Harry and I'm so happy for him and his beautiful family, but I have very little in common with him and when he runs out of conversation he usually reverts to the jokes. When Mum and Dad were around, I could hide behind them, so to speak. Now, spending time with Harry is draining, using my defences at full force to keep up the show that none of his '*jokes*' bother me. That's why I haven't visited much. Why I'm nearly a stranger to my nephews when Jake is practically a third parent.

"What are the road closures about outside?" I ask, trying to do my part and make polite conversation.

"The fair tomorrow," Lisa says.

"Fair?" Jake asks and Lisa rolls her eyes.

"It's on the itinerary, Jake," she says with affectionate frustration.

"Nel," Jake gasps with mock horror. "With all that studying of the itinerary we did this morning, I still can't recite the damn thing."

I hide my smile behind my hand before schooling my features and looking at him with as much disappointment I can muster. "Well, your study methods are quite lacking, Mr. Partridge."

His eyes flash with mischief and that Elvis smile tugs his lips on one side.

"Babe," Lisa whines to Harry. "They're making fun of my itinerary."

Harry reaches his hand to his wife with wide eyes. "I don't know why, my dear. It's *such* a normal thing to do!" His sarcasm has the whole room chuckling. Lisa punches his arm but leans into him, trying to pout over her smile.

"Oh, my darling," Charles laughs at his daughter. "We all very much appreciate your organisation and everything you have done to look after us this Christmas."

Cheers erupt around the room.

Jake's eyes catch mine and a slow and sexy smile stretches his lips. For a brief moment my skin heats thinking of him looming over me under that mistletoe, how I thought he might have kissed me if I hadn't moved away. Man, I wish I knew for sure.

"Right," Lisa says, with a clap of her hands. "The boys have asked that we play a game before dinner."

"Yes!" Oscar jumps from Harry's lap.

"And what exactly are we playing, kiddos?" Gordan asks.

"Hide and seek!" Lucas says, jumping up.

The adults all chuckle.

"I'm too old to play hide and seek," Hen laughs.

"No you're not!" Oscar defends, pulling at her hands to get her standing. "You lot all hide and Lucas and I will find you. Whoever finds the most people wins."

"And whoever is the last person to be found wins for the hiders," Jake announces, standing up, and holding little Margot out for Lis to take.

"Well, I'm too big to hide anywhere, and someone needs to look after the little ones," Lisa says, pulling Freddie from Lucas.

"What's our countdown, Ozzy?" Jake asks, bouncing from one foot to the other, punching the air like Rocky. I smile at the nickname; I thought I was the only one who called Oscar that.

"Thirty seconds," Oscar answers and before anyone has a chance to get up, Lucas starts counting loudly.

The older generation grunt and groan trying to get off the sofas, but Jake darts out the room, more excited than the kids.

Lucas is just past fifteen as I get upstairs, Lisa says we can use rooms that the doors are open of, which basically rules out Rhiannon and Luke's room. I debate the bathroom, but Harry and Lisa don't have cheap shower curtains, but transparent shower cubicles. I need to find somewhere to hide, and I admit to having a flutter of nerves in my belly as I think. Just like when you're a kid. The smile stretching my face is probably the easiest that's come since we started the holiday. This is fun.

Lisa's parents and Aunt and Uncle all stayed downstairs; I have no idea where Jake went as he was out the door before any of us knew what was happening. Harry rushes past me in the hall and opens a door to a rather large airing cupboard.

"Come on Nelly-Belly," he whisper-shouts at me. "Get a wriggle on."

He slides between two shelving units and shuts the door behind him. I panic when I hear Lucas scream *THIRTY* at the top of his lungs. I dart into the nearest bedroom, which I can only assume is Lisa and Harry's because it's huge. Decorated in soft pinks and greys with the biggest bed I've ever seen. I open a door to the left and see a large walk-in wardrobe. I close the door behind me but hesitate in the middle, deciding which side I should hide behind when an arm flings out and snakes around my waist, pulling me through a wall of evening gowns.

CHAPTER NINE
"I'm not above sabotage, you know?"

JAKE

Harry and Lisa are total couple-goals. I'm man enough to admit that I'm a little jealous of my best friend. They were always the perfect couple, perfect jobs, perfect kids, perfect house. And now, on Christmas Eve-Eve in their home that the McCallisters would be proud of, I'm playing hide and seek like a big kid. Harry gets to join in, too, while his wife entertains her niece and nephew. He has it made. It's never worked out for me. Girlfriends and I have always wanted different things. Plus, there was always the issue of anytime a relationship started getting serious, a certain set of chocolate-brown eyes seemed to haunt me.

I'll admit I always thought Nel was cute but in a sweet younger sister kind of way. When she got older, I certainly noticed how pretty she was, but she was still shy and retiring and I felt more protective than attracted. It wasn't until I started seeing her online that something changed. I became intrigued by the person on the screen and definitely felt an attraction then. And I know how that sounds, okay. I have *not* been jerking it to pictures of my best friend's little sister. It's not even the photos of her half naked arranged elegantly on plush furniture that had me hooked. It's the videos where she's talking to the camera. When she gives her followers that big, unhindered smile and talks freely and confidently. My favourite are the makeup tutorials—yes, I watch makeup tutorials, don't be weird about it, okay?—where it's just her, a ring light, and her art. She talks to the audience about her day, her clients, and what she's doing.

She is mesmerising. She's cute and funny and her laugh sends pangs through my chest. How come I never heard that laugh before?

I want to get to know the Nel in those videos. She's been plaguing me and my relationships for three years, and this morning I woke up with her arse firmly in my palm. Then a ten-minute car journey smelling her sweet scent drove me to make a risky decision, caging her against the car. I had to walk away before I did something really stupid like kiss her. Her lips are so plump and painted a deep pink that, in my head, tastes of sweet berries. Also, there was that glimpse of something red and lacy in her suitcase last night. Now, I have to say, I *really* like women in lingerie. I'm sure most men would say that but then when they have a beautiful woman in front of them wearing intricate pieces, they'd be in a hurry to get her naked. I don't want to rid a woman of a perfect ensemble; I like to work round it. There's something about seeing soft silk against soft skin, delicate lace against delicate flesh, it sends all the blood rushing to my cock. Okay, yes, the makeup videos intrigue me, but the photographs turn me absolutely feral.

I have exactly one minute to think about all of this from my cushty hiding spot before the door to Lisa's fancy walk-in opens and closes gently. I don't have to poke my head out to see who it is, that brown sugar and sweet cinnamon scent fills the small space. I peak between the hangers and see her standing in the middle of the cupboard, looking indecisive. Her long, light-brown hair hangs in a thick braid all the way down to the middle of her back, and she looks effortlessly fashionable in her bright blue jeans and white shirt. I smile to myself as she just stands there. As the pitter patter of small feet come rushing up the stairs, I grab her and pull her to the dark side of the closet.

"You moving in on my prime hiding spot, Forrest?" I tease with narrowed eyes. Although it may have come out a little more threatening than planned, as there is a lot less room back here since I have her pushed against the wall; I'm nearly plastered against her and no space to move.

She arches a manicured brow at me and purses her juicy lips. "I didn't know you were here, *Partridge*."

"Hmmm," I make the sound suspicious and subconsciously—yes, definitely subconsciously—I press into her a little further. "I'm not above sabotage, you know?"

Her eyes widen in mock shock. "I thought you had some making up to do. You know, I may have to see a specialist about my back, I'm getting a little shoulder pain." She rolls her neck as though to test her discomfort and lets out a groan that has me nearly forgetting our little game. My cock twitches and I have to move my hips to try and save her from feeling the extent of my perversion.

"This is war, sweetheart." I lean in, to hover my lips over hers and rest my forearm on the wall above her head. "But if you're a good girl, I'll rub you all better tonight."

The satisfaction I feel in the way her eyes widen is better than anything, and her gasp comes just as the door swings open. I place a finger over my lips to remind her to keep quiet as one of the boys rummages through clothes on the other side of the closet. She bites her lip to stop her smile and, fuck me, I want to sink my teeth into that lip. So, I do the only thing I can think of, I push her back out to the other side of the rails.

"Aunty Nels-Bells?" Oscar's surprise nearly makes me laugh and give myself away.

"Hey, Ozzy," Nel puffs.

"Why'd you jump out at me? I'm supposed to find you." His highly suspicious tone is highly comical.

"Oh, I thought we were meant to scare the people looking for us," she answers, perfectly.

I can practically hear Oscar rolling his eyes. "Well, I found you now. You can go and wait in the lounge with everyone else.

Just Dad and Uncle Jake left to find. They're not in there with you, are they?"

"Nope," she answers immediately, popping the p and I smile to myself.

Good girl.

Dinner is another feat of culinary expertise. Steak and ale pie with the creamiest, smoothest, fluffiest mashed potatoes I have ever tasted, along with vegetables and gravy. When we sit down, Nel stares disbelieving at the spread and seems to draw in on herself. She's sat next to me today, so I put my palm on her thigh and lean in.

"Are you okay?"

She starts to nod but then looks at me and seems to make a decision. "This is my mum's steak and ale pie. She always made it at Christmas."

I smile and squeeze her leg in what I'm hoping is a reassuring and not a creepy gesture. As much as Nel had a schoolgirl crush on me fifteen years ago, I know she's grown so much since she started living in the city and I can't assume that my contact is wanted. She doesn't seem to mind though; her eyes are glassy as she looks at me. "That's why it's so good."

She nods and a single tear drops to her cheek. I want to wipe it away, but she turns away before I can tell myself it's a bad idea. Harry places a gravy boat on the table and squeezes Nel's shoulder as he passes, planting a quick kiss on her hair.

"Lisa wanted to do something for you," he whispers to her and Nel smiles through tears. "Make sure you thank her."

I roll my eyes, as if Nel needs reminding to be polite. Apparently, Harry has to ruin every nice moment he has with Nel. She nods and wipes her tears, digging into the small plate she's dished herself up. I wait, wanting to watch her and it doesn't disappoint. Her eyes close as she takes her first bite and moans around her mouthful, chewing slowly and deliberately.

Yep, it's official; I have a crush on my best friend's little sister.

Dinner progresses in a blur of friendly conversation and alcohol, but I'm too focussed on Nel to take part in any of it. Before this gathering, I knew I found her attractive; have for years, even before all the social media posts. I knew I wanted to get to know her again after I started lightly cyber-stalking her, but I didn't realise I wanted her until I started spending time with her again. She is exquisite.

"You enjoying that?" I ask with an indulgent smile.

"Oh my God, it's so good." She sits back and looks at me with a giant grin. "I think these potatoes may even be better than Dad's. His were always a little lumpy."

"I remember," I chuckle.

"I miss them, Jake." Her smile remains but her eyes grow sad, looking down at her empty plate.

"I know, sweetheart." She blinks in surprise at the term of endearment. "I miss them too, you know?"

She nods, holding my gaze with her own. "I guess they were kind of your second parents too, huh?"

I nod, smiling at the memories of Mary and Carl looking out for me like one of their own. My parents worked a lot, so my summers and a couple evenings a week for most of my childhood were spent at the Forrests'. Carl insisted that Harry and I learn to cook, do laundry, and often had us helping with chores while he made sure Nel could change the wheel on the car in the event of a flat. Mary was a fusser, she was always checking that we were fed, watered, warm, comfortable. The Forrests were always playing boardgames or doing family days out. They spent their time together and doted on Harry and Nel. My parents are wonderful but their evenings after gruelling workdays were spent in front of the TV, and weekends were for chores. We had the occasional holiday, and my sister and I got along fine. I had a happy childhood in a loving family. But I can't deny that the Forrests were as much my family as the Partridges.

When Harry called me to say that his Mum had died unexpectedly, I was with him straight away. I held him as he cried and let my own tears fall to his shoulder. I thought of Nel then, how she would be heartbroken, how she should have been with us.

"I think they'd be pleased you were spending Christmas with us this year." Nel's sweet voice draws me back to the present and I smile at her sentiment, knowing that what she said was true.

"I think so too." I realise that we are so close the tips of our noses barely scraping each other.

She inhales deeply and sits back in her seat, putting some distance back between us. I do the same and try to swallow my heart which seems to be trying to pump its way up my throat. I look up to find Lisa watching on with amused interest. *What?* I mouth at her, and she just shrugs and goes back to pretending she was listening to the conversation between Rhiannon and Hen.

"Are you really having more potatoes, Nelly-Belly? Hope you brought your stretchy pants," Harry snorts, taking a long gulp of wine.

Once again, Nel freezes with potato halfway to her plate. No one laughs with Harry as he goes back to his conversation with Charles about something boring. When no one is watching, Nel slowly puts the serving spoon with the small dollop of mashed potato back into the serving dish and sits back in her chair with her shoulders hunched, trying to make herself small. With a huff of annoyance, I reach over and scoop a healthy portion of potato from the dish and put it on her plate.

"Eat, enjoy the meal Lis made especially for you."

She hesitates only for a moment before digging in and I sit with my arm resting on the back of her chair, feeling overly protective and trying desperately not to let it slip to rest on her back instead. Thou shalt not covet thy best friend's little sister, after all.

CHAPTER TEN
"Dude, she's kind of incredible."

JAKE

"Can Aunty Nel read to us tonight?" Oscar asks when both he and Lucas come down in their matching Christmas pyjamas to say goodnight. The fear in Nel's eyes at this prospect is hilarious, she looks like she's just been asked to explain String Theory.

"Only if Aunty Nel is happy with that," Lisa answers softly and everyone's eyes turn to Nel. I hide my laughter behind the crystal tumbler holding my Old Fashioned. I'm glad that we'll be getting a taxi tonight so I can let the alcohol magnify this moment.

"Uh, yeah. Okay, sure," Nel says, nodding as though trying to encourage herself. She gets up to follow her nephews up the stairs, but turns to Harry and Lisa, her face screwed up in question. "Do I need to do anything? Do they need milk or something?"

I snort. I can't help it.

Harry frowns at her. "They're six and nine."

She blinks at him waiting for further explanation but when it doesn't come, she says, "So, no?"

Lisa smiles kindly and speaks gently. "They don't have milk, just head on up and they'll show you what to do. But don't let them bully you into reading a third book. Two max."

She nods, looking like she's trying to lock those instructions in her brain and follows the boys up the stairs. Lisa starts getting up to clear the table but Harry puts his palm on her hand, stopping her.

65

"Go sit down, babe. Put your feet up and relax. Jake and I'll wash up."

I nod at her in confirmation and see her shoulders relax in gratitude. "Yeah, go on, *babe*." I grin at her, and she throws a rolled-up napkin at me.

As Lisa retreats to the living room, taking everyone else with her, Harry and I stack plates. I roll up the sleeves of my t-shirt and fill the sink. We fall into comfortable silence, working together to clear the minimal mess that Lisa made cooking.

"How you doing, H?" I ask, concentrating on the saucepan I'm washing as he loads the dishwasher with the plates.

"I'm great," he says with a forced air of ease.

"Harry," I press.

He sighs, standing straight and looking at me. I hold his gaze, waiting for him to figure out his feelings. "I'm okay. Lis has been running around trying to do everything—to make everything perfect—and doesn't want me doing much because she thinks I'm going to break down or something." He runs his hand through his styled blonde hair, effectively messing it up. "I'd rather she relaxed a bit and concentrates on growing that baby."

"Are you?" I ask gently.

"Am I what?"

"Going to break down?" I abandon the saucepan and turn to face him. Giving him my full attention. "You haven't really taken time to grieve, H."

He huffs a laugh, looking down to his shoe. "You sound like Lisa."

"Good, she's a very smart woman," I say. "Just don't tell her I said that."

He looks at me with a grin. "She already knows she's smarter than you, Partridge."

"I'm sure she does," I laugh. "So come on, stop deflecting. Are you okay?"

He leans back on the counter and folds his arms over his chest. "I don't know, honestly. I feel like I need to keep going for my family. Lis is seven months pregnant and still refusing to slow down. The last thing she needs is for me to stop functioning. The boys were so upset to lose Dad but we'd talked them through it beforehand so they were prepared. But with Mum going just like that, it threw them through a loop. They still get teary and I need to be able to hold them through it."

I take in a deep breath and level with him, "You ever think that maybe they need you to cry too, mate? So they know it's okay to grieve?" He clenches his jaw and swallows; I can see the thin glaze of moisture in his eyes and reach to squeeze his shoulder. "You know I'm not telling you how to parent—"

"I know," he gives me a half smile. "I'm just…"

I squeeze his shoulder again, encouraging him to continue. When he doesn't, I say, "You're just what?"

"I'm scared, Jake." That moisture now pools in the rim of his eyes. "I'm scared that if I let myself break, there won't be any coming back from it."

"Dude, no matter how much you break, there are people willing to put you back together again." He scrubs his palm over his face, erasing the evidence of tears, and takes a deep breath through his nose. "Lisa may need you right now, but it's okay for you to need her too, mate. She's a tough cookie, she can handle looking after you a little bit. You know I'm here for you, H. I'll hold you while you cry, or I'll take the kids off your hands so you can have time to yourself or with Lis. Nel's going through it too, I'm sure she'd be here for you."

He lets out a humourless laugh, turning round to continue loading the dishwasher. "I don't know what's going on with her."

"What do you mean?" I frown down at him as he's bent over dirty dishes.

He sighs, shaking his head. "She completely shut down at the funerals and couldn't handle anything. I had to do it all and since then, she's not wanted to see me or do anything. I was in the city to sort out probate with her and she wouldn't even come to lunch. I had to practically beg her to come here for Christmas. She would rather be spending the holiday alone than with me." His lip twitches like he's fighting his emotions again. "I feel like now Mum and Dad are gone; she's done with me."

"That's not true, Harry." I mean, Nel hasn't exactly told me otherwise, but I can't imagine that being her attitude.

"I worry about her, Jake." I can see the worry in his eyes and the tense set of his jaw. "She's so quiet and shy, she was still really dependent on Mum and Dad and now they're gone. She's going to close in on herself and become a hermit."

I screw my face up, confused by that prediction. Nel is quiet, sure, but she's outgoing in her profession, she's popular and well liked. She talks about friends in her videos, she does tutorials before heading out for dinner or drinks with them. "I don't think you should worry too much, H. She needs you to be her brother, not her parent. Nel's an adult who's more than capable to live her life, but maybe she could use a partner in her grief."

He shrugs and won't meet my eye. "Hard to do when she doesn't want to spend time with me."

I internally debate the best way to say the next thing. "Have you thought that maybe she doesn't want to spend time with you because you're constantly making fun of her?"

It's his turn to look confused. "What do you mean?"

"Dude," I groan. "You've been making jokes at her expense since she showed up."

"No, I haven't!"

"Yes, you have." I pull the plug from the sink, the washing up done, and Harry closes the dishwasher. "Mate, I love you, but you go a little bit cuckoo in front of Lisa's folks and Nel seems to be taking the brunt of it. You keep making jokes about what she's eating, you get all cagey whenever her job comes up, and you tell her off like one of the boys if she does something you don't agree with."

He just stares at me, clearly not convinced.

"You need to lighten up, mate. Nel isn't a porn star. Not that there is anything wrong with that, and not that you could judge considering the movies I saw on your laptop in college." I chuckle when he narrows his eyes and glares daggers at me. "She's created her own brand and is making a living encouraging women to love themselves no matter their insecurities. Dude, she's kind of incredible."

His eyes widen in surprise at that statement, and I can feel my cheeks heat a little, thinking I may have overshared. "You follow her? You've seen the stuff she posts?"

I shrug it off as no big deal and lie through my teeth. "Just one or two here and there. Have *you* actually looked at the stuff she does?"

He screws his face up. "Dude, I don't want to see my sister in her underwear."

I roll my eyes. "There's other stuff there too, H. Listen, you don't have to look into it if you don't want to, but don't judge what you don't understand. And don't assume Nel needs you to look after her. She's doing good and you two are equals, yeah? Tell her how you're feeling and let her do the same. You two should have each other right now."

He nods slowly and I feel a little flutter of satisfaction that he seems to be taking on board what I'm saying. "I'll take it under advisement," he smiles at me. I place both my hands on his shoulders this time and level him with a serious look.

"I mean it though, Harry. You need me, I'm here. Don't be afraid to lean on the people around you."

Instead of answering, he pulls me in to a fierce hug and slaps my back.

"Oh sorry!" A sweet voice from the doorway breaks us apart. Nel stands there looking awkward. "I uh, didn't mean to interrupt. Uh, where is everyone?"

"In the lounge," Harry says, clapping me on the back. "We're just coming. Did the boys go down okay?" He puts his arm around her shoulders as he leads her to the living room.

The sweet smile she gives him has my heart pumping that little bit harder. She doesn't want to cut him out, she just wants his kindness. "Yep, all good. They're such great kids, Harry. I'm so proud of you, and them."

He leans back to look down at her, a huge smile spreading across his lips. "Thank you. I love you, little sister." He squeezes her and plants a kiss on her hair.

Charles, Cami, Gordan, and Hen only make it to ten before they call it a night. Drinks keep flowing though, and I'm completely relaxed, enjoying the company.

"Oh God," Rhiannon moans, once her parents have been gone for a few minutes. "Tell me I can go out for a smoke now."

"You smoke?" I ask.

"Not if my parents ask," she smiles at me, wiggling her eyebrows and I laugh.

"You're how old? And you have to hide from your mum and dad?"

"Twenty-nine and three quarters. And yes."

"I got you, babe." Luke stands, holding out two cigarettes.

Lisa looks at Harry. "You want to go out with them?"

He looks a little nervous, rubbing the back of his neck staring at Nel. "I uh, I have the two Cuban cigars Dad had left. I was going to have one this weekend, would you like the other?"

"*Me?*" She stares at him in disbelief.

"Who else?" He smiles at her. "Come on, Nelly-Belly. Let's go." He stands and holds his hand out to her as we all pile outside.

It turns out Nel does not like cigars. After two puffs and a lot of coughing and spluttering, she hands it to me to finish it off with Harry, who is savouring his own. We sit on their garden furniture in the cold, wrapped up in scarves and hats, Lisa staying upwind of the smoke and enjoying another hour of conversation. Harry is relaxed and easy going. Nel sits with Rhiannon and talks about her work with passion and enthusiasm. The evening is perfect.

When Lisa finally decides she's had enough, she says goodnight and heads to bed, quickly followed by Rhiannon. Nel throws me a look that silently asks if I'm ready to go, so I start saying goodbye and the grateful smile she gives me has me staring at her lips.

Harry and Luke stay outside as we head our way through the house to the porch. Nel stops under the door to pull her hat further down before we leave. I see that sprig of mistletoe directly above her head and when she sees me, her gaze follows mine until she's craning her neck to look up. It has to be the booze that moves my feet forward. I'll blame the martini I had before dinner for stepping up to her until we're toe-to-toe. I can attribute my hands reaching to cup her face to the wine I had with my meal, and the Old Fashioned is definitely responsible for my lips covering hers. She gasps into my mouth and the sound shoots straight to my dick. I gently kiss her, testing the seam of her lips with the tip of my tongue. When she melts into me, opening her mouth and welcoming my invasion, I take and take.

She whimpers and I groan as lips and tongues move together in lust and need and we pull apart panting just as the sound of the back door opening reaches us. Nel's hand flies to her mouth, touching her lips and staring at me in disbelief. I stare back a prickle of guilt scurrying over the back of my neck. I shouldn't have done that.

71

CHAPTER ELEVEN
"You want all these whips out?"

NEL

O ur journey back to the hotel is completely silent. Jake's kiss still burning at my lips and the soft pressure of his palm still pressing against my jaw. It isn't until we're walking in through the lobby that I realise neither of us asked Lisa and Harry if one of us could stay on their couch. It seems after a brief discussion about it this morning, neither of us are actually bothered about our sleeping situation. We head up to our room and continue not talking to each other as we move around, getting ready to call it a night. Jake is already in bed, scrolling on his phone but I've only just removed my makeup and moisturised my face. I flip open my case to retrieve the pyjamas I'd shoved in there this morning and once again, my red lace bra and panty set is exposed to the room.

I don't immediately shut the case this time, but I do turn to Jake to see if he saw anything. I find him staring at me with heavy lidded eyes and his expression dark. My tongue darts out to wet my lips and I swallow over my dry throat.

"Can I ask you something personal?" he says, cocking his head to one side and breaking the silence.

"Sure," I croak, closing the case and standing.

"Did you bring that because that's what you usually wear under your clothes, or were you planning on modelling it?"

I am *not* embarrassed by what I do, but for some reason, I blush and look to the carpet. "Uh…well, I didn't know we would be sharing a room."

"I'm sorry I won't get to see it."

"I uh…what?"

"The post, I mean." His amused smirk sends flutters through my belly and lower.

Is he flirting? I've seen Jake flirt with a lot of girls and have been so sure that I'd never be on the receiving end of it that my flirt receptors may be off. I mean, he did kiss me. But that was probably just so he didn't get seven years' bad luck. *Or did we agree that was just mirrors?* Hang on, what did he just say? Should I be speaking?

Jake chuckles. "Relax, Nel."

"I was planning on doing some photos here. I saw the hotel online and the rooms are really beautiful." I gesture to the chic botanical wallpaper and lush velvet bedding. "I thought they would be a good setting to take some pictures, but it's cool. I'll do them another time." I shrug and the twinge in my shoulder reminds me that my back is still sore.

Jake must see the pain in my face as he frowns and sits forward. "You *are* hurt?"

"I'm fine, Jake. Don't fuss." I wave him off.

"Go get changed," he commands softly and my head jerks back at the sudden change of conversation.

I do as he says, changing in the privacy of the bathroom and trotting back to deposit my clothes back in my case. I pull the covers back to get into bed, but Jake pats the mattress by his leg. "Sit."

With a raised brow, I do as I'm told and scooch over to sit next to him. At the first feel of his fingers on my bare shoulder, I gasp and turn to look at him. "What are you doing?"

"I told you I'd rub it all better." His voice seems to have dropped an octave as he watches his thumb knead my aching muscles.

My heart is thumping against my breastbone, hard enough to judder my whole body. "Jake, I…" I trail off because I don't know what to say. I should tell him to stop because my stupid heart will start getting stupid ideas. I should say I'm fine and that we should just go to sleep because every brush of his skin against mine is like lightning in my veins and I don't want to fully turn back into that sad schoolgirl pining over her brother's best friend with not a chance in Hell of having him.

"You want me to stop, Nel?" His voice is low and steady and much closer than I thought. His lips close to my ear, sending shivers down my spine. "Just tell me you don't want this."

This? *This?* What's this? He means just the massage, right?

I can't tell him to stop, the warmth of his hands on my skin won't let me. "It feels really good," I say breathily instead.

"Well, hopefully this makes us even for me knocking you on your arse," he says far more upbeat and chummier than before and I just nod, feeling a moment I couldn't quite grasp has passed. He only touches the top of my back and my shoulders, not venturing any lower. *Because he isn't attracted to you, stupid girl. He just wanted to make up for your fall...and kissed you silly.*

"Thanks, I think I'm good now." I move away from him and slide into bed. "I should probably get to sleep, I've got to be up and out early."

He looks at me in question.

"I'm heading back into London tomorrow; I've got a client at nine o'clock and I don't have an assistant, so I need to be there early enough to set up."

"I could be your assistant." He looks as surprised by his words as I am.

"You don't have to do that."

"I want to," he says, sliding to lay down and turning on his side to face me. "Let me come and watch you work."

"O-okay."

*****

74

It's only a forty-minute train journey to Waterloo and then two tubes to my little studio situated above a Lebanese restaurant. Even this early in the morning when the restaurant is closed, the smell of sweet spices and mint permeates the air. I switch the heaters on as soon as we get inside. When taking photographs of people in their underwear, it is important to keep things toasty. It takes only a few minutes to get the place nice and warm, so I shed my hat, gloves, and coat.

"You want a coffee?" Jake asks, pointing his thumb over his shoulder. "I saw a Starbucks up the road."

"Oh, don't go there," I say as I screw my face up. "There's a little café just opposite that does the best chai tea latte."

"One of those then?" he asks with a smile and I nod.

While he's gone, I set up my camera and my lights. I have two sets that I use: one with a large metal framed four poster bed draped in wispy, white fabric and several sets of sheets in varying colours. The other is an empty corner with exposed brick walls that I can put a backdrop up or move any of the random props or pieces of furniture into. In the opposite corner, I have a tiny kitchenette with a single cupboard, one drawer, a mini fridge, a kettle, and a microwave. By the stairs from the front door, I have a couple of chairs and a coffee table. And off to one side is a dressing table with one of those antique looking room dividers that clients can change behind. It isn't much, no more than one room but I worked hard to get it looking good, with a lot of help from my dad. In just a few years, I have used this space to build a successful business.

I look around my baby, my sanctuary, and think back on Charles' words from yesterday. *I'm sure your parents were incredibly proud too. I would be.* For the first time, I try to see myself and my life from their eyes, not comparing it to those around me, not choosing to focus on what I need to do better, but just looking at what I have done. And I smile. Charles is right, they were proud of me. They saw me achieve something I'm so happy with, and they were proud.

I'm still smiling to myself when Jake walks in. Is there a more beautiful sight in the world than a gorgeous man carrying sweet, caffeinated goodness your way? He gives me that sexy Elvis smile and a lock of his dark brown hair falls over his eyes in a way that makes me want to roll the silky strand between my fingers.

"Thank you." I bring the cup to my lips and sip the aromatic chai, nodding when it hits the spot. I catch Jake staring at me, his eyes trailing my lips as my tongue catches a drop of tea from them. He seems to shake himself out of whatever thoughts that are occupying his head and looks around.

"So, what do you need help with?"

"Um," I look around too. "I haven't had a chance to chat to this client much before today, it was kind of a rushed appointment. So I don't know what they're going to want." I bite my lip in thought. "Could you open up that cabinet over there?" I point to the far wall where I keep most of my props. "And get the stuff out and ready?"

He heads over to the cabinet while I start arranging the curtains around the bed to how I like them, then set up the backdrop so it can be easily rolled in if we need it.

"Um, Nel?"

"Hmm?"

"You want all these whips out?"

I turn to see him smirking at me with a cherry red riding crop in one hand, slapping it against the palm of the other. Salacious thoughts stop my brain from functioning for a moment. *Very* salacious thoughts.

Jake isn't deterred by my lack of response, approaching slowly with the crop still in hand. "You like this kind of stuff?"

I clear my throat and some of my thoughts. "It's not about what *I* like, it's about what the client wants."

"Hmm," he pouts thoughtfully and leans down so we're close, speaking in a soft rumble, "But *do* you like it?"

I can't help my mouth tugging into a smile and I'm debating whether to answer that when the bell above the door sounds, signalling that my client has arrived. I take a step back from man currently causing my brain to short circuit and plaster a customer friendly smile on my face. Footsteps thud up the creaky, old, wooden stairs and in my peripheral vision I see Jake's eyebrows shoot up when my client reaches us with a nervous smile.

CHAPTER TWELVE
"Why do you want to kiss me, Jake?"

JAKE

"**M**r. Owuo, it's so nice to finally meet you." Nel steps forward stretching out her hand to the *man* who just walked in. I was not expecting a dude. I was expecting a woman and planning on sitting on the comfy chairs at the front, not watching the shoot like some creeper.

"Please, call me Micha." The guy has a rich and smooth voice but there's a definite twinge of nerves in the background. He's probably in his late forties or early fifties with brown skin and a goatee peppered with grey despite his shortly clipped hair still being completely black.

"Micha," Nel says with a warm smile. "I'm so glad we were able to get this booked in.

"Yeah," he smiles somewhat shyly, rubbing the back of his neck. "Thank you so much for fitting me in on Christmas Eve. I'm sorry to be so awkward, it's just difficult with work and finding time to sneak off without my wife knowing."

Without his wife knowing? That sounds dodgy. What does he think is going to happen here? I take an instinctual step toward Nel.

"Ah, yes. I understand." Nel chuckles, completely comfortable. "I'm guessing this is all going to be a surprise for your wife?"

Oh, wait. Yeah, no. That makes more sense. Jeesh, cool it, Partridge.

"Yeah." He smiles, clearly thinking of his wife.

"Micha, this is my friend Jake." Nel gestures toward me. "He came with me this morning just to help get set up. Now, he can stay to help me move things around to keep things running smoothly so we finish in good time, or I can ask him to step out if you'd be more comfortable with just the two of us."

Micha looks at me and I can see the fear in his eyes. I kind of feel bad for the guy but also wonder why on earth he's here if he doesn't want to be. Completely expecting him to want me gone, I'm just about to say that I'll head back to the café when he speaks up.

"I think it would be best if he stays, if that's okay?" I blink at him for a second and then nod. "It's just a bit weird to be parading around in my underwear in front of a young woman I hardly know, might be a bit less weird if there's another guy here."

Nel chuckles, "Sure. Here, why don't you take a seat, and we'll figure out what you want to get out of today." They take the two seats either side of the coffee table to chat while I stand awkwardly to one side, still reeling from the fact that there is a guy here to have a sexy photoshoot. I'm pretty sure I've seen all of Nel's posts—yes, we've established I'm slightly stalker-y, let's not keep going on about it—and I'm pretty sure I've never seen a guy on there. I mean, I know she doesn't post all of her clients, but most of them are middle aged women and a fair few younger women. I'm tempted to get my phone out to double check if I've seen a guy on there before, but that would probably be rude.

They talk briefly about why Micha is here—he wants to gift his wife the photos for Valentine's Day—and what he wants to do in the photos. The look on his face when she mentions the props has me smothering a laugh behind my palm.

"Okay, so no whips or handcuffs," Nel determines.

"Uh, no," he agrees bashfully. "I don't want to look stupid," he almost whispers.

Nel tilts her head and smiles warmly at the man. "I won't let that happen. I promise, this is going to be really cool."

"Have you photographed men before?" he asks.

"Oh God, yeah," she snorts, pulling a leather-bound folder from the bottom of the table and flicks through it until she finds the page she's looking for and turns it to him. I crane my neck to look too, completely fascinated with all of this. There in the portfolio, is a collection of photos of men. There's one who must be a model, if he isn't he should change careers. The guy is in his mid-twenties with an impeccable body, brooding at the camera like he's commanding it to join him in the bed he's lounging on. The others are normal people. Older guys, beer bellies, skinny ones, and even one dressed as Batman. Micha and I must both spot that one at the same time as we each look to Nel with a raised brow in question.

She just smirks with a shrug. "Hey, I don't judge."

Just a few more minutes of conversation and Nel instructs Micha to go behind the screen and get ready, which he does, blowing out a big breath like he can expel his nerves with the air. She asks me to help her pull a red sheet over the mattress and add some light fabric to the frame in the same shade, along with the white curtains already there. Micha comes out from behind the screen, looking highly uncomfortable in nothing but a pair of black boxers.

I step back as Nel instructs him how to position himself on the bed. It's nothing overtly sexual; first she has him leaning against the wall where there would normally be a headboard but there isn't, then she tells him to sit on the edge of the bed with his elbows resting on his thighs. I stand behind Nel as she snaps away and then checks the photos on her digital camera. Micha's nerves are the only thing showing on the little screen. His smile is forced, and his eyes are terrified. I'm no artist, but I can tell these aren't great.

"Micha, why are you doing this for your wife?" Nel asks as she snaps another photo. When he just looks at her in confusion, she says, "Why do you think she'd like this as a Valentine's gift?"

"Oh," he says, looking at his hands. "She actually came to you a couple years ago."

"She did?" Nel lowers her camera and then her face lights up in recognition. "Carla?" When he nods, she chuckles. "I should have put two and two together when I heard your surname." She heads to the wall with the dressing table which has framed photos of about twenty different women from shoots and plucks one from the wall. She quickly shows me before handing it to Micha. A beautiful woman who seems a little younger than Micha lays on the very bed he's sat on, her smooth skin practically glowing in the lights. The photo is in black and white so the focus is purely on her as she stretches her body over the mattress and stares at the camera with what can only be described as *bedroom eyes*.

Micha's eyes shine and his smile stretches wide as he takes the picture from Nel. "That's her, my Carla."

"So, she came to me and then you thought you'd do the same?" Nel pushes, her camera clicking as Micha looks at the photo of his wife.

"Well, her photos were..." he pushes out a long breath and continues, "amazing. I have one in my wallet that she caught me looking at a while back and said that she would love to have some sexy photos to look at too." There's that squirming shyness again.

"Can we try something?" Nel says and Micha nods.

She asks me to grab the stepladder tucked away by the cabinet where the whips were, which I do. By the time I get back, Micha is laying in the bed, the cherry red sheets bunched and draped around him like they've been slept in, and the photo of his wife is laid at an angle by his head.

"Do you and your wife lay in on a Sunday morning, Micha?"

"Yeah."

"What do you guys talk about in those moments?"

He chuckles and bites his lip as he thinks, a shy smirk telling us that the answer may not be safe for work. Before he gives his answer, Nel is clicking her camera.

"Ah ha! I know that look," she smiles down at him. "Micha these photos are coming out great, look at your wife's picture." He does. "That's how good you look too."

Snap. Snap. Snap.

They move to the other set and do some more concepts, use some props—not whips—and I watch in fascination. At Nel, obviously. Micha's fine but I really don't swing that way. He came in this morning like a kid who'd been sent to the principal's office for the first time, but she put him at ease quickly and gently. Far from the mouse she's been at her brother's, she is calm and assertive as she directs her client. She checks the screen on her camera often and she gives him encouragement, telling him how great the pictures are coming out. He is so different from the man who walked in, and she is the woman I've been watching on Instagram for years and dying to meet.

Micha is there for an hour before he dresses and thanks Nel profusely with a handshake that turns into a hug. When she showed him some of the shots on her camera he huffed an amazed laugh, clapping his palm over his mouth and I can't help but smile with him. Another hug with Nel and a shake of my hand and he leaves us to tidy up. I pack all the—no less than seven—whips back in the prop cabinet and have a little poke around. There's a bag full of Christmas decorations, on top of which is a plastic sprig of mistletoe. I roll the stem between my fingers, recalling my ill-advised actions of last night. The thing is, the more I think about it, the less regretful I become. I mean, I'm not some creeper—despite what you may think—and I'm not taking advantage of Nel. I'm not interested in messing her around, but the more time I spend with her, the clearer it's becoming that I want her. I want to start something. Something real and, although I know in my heart of hearts that Harry won't just give us a thumbs up and let it be, I find myself not giving a flying fuck.

In the time it's taken me to gather my thoughts, Nel has packed away the backdrop and stripped the sheets from the bed. I stand with the mistletoe in my hand and walk over to her, her head snaps to me and her eyes find the sprig.

"What are you doing?"

"I'm going to kiss you, but I brought props in case you need an excuse."

Her lips twitch as I stop just in front of her. "Jake, I…" her words trail off and she looks down, uncertainty clouding her pretty brown eyes.

"You don't want to kiss me?" I try for a teasing tone but my own insecurity bites at my heart. Nel had a crush on me years ago, but I may have been reading her wrong the last couple of days.

"I…"

Shit. I *have* read this wrong. I take a step back and clear my throat. "I'm sorry. I uh…I shouldn't have—"

"Why do you want to kiss me, Jake?" She cocks her head to one side and narrows her eyes in confusion.

Jesus, am I sweating? "I uh…I thought there was something…" I clear my throat feeling uncharacteristically embarrassed. "Um, something between us."

"Oh." Her eyes pop wide. "You did?"

"You didn't?" I frown.

"I don't know. I guess I never allowed myself to believe there was anything from your side."

I eat up the distance between us again and cup her jaw, the mistletoe still between my fingers. "Why?"

"Because you're Jake and I'm—"

"Perfect," I finish for her before planting a soft kiss on her lips.

83

CHAPTER THIRTEEN:
"We could all use a little Christmas spirit all year round."

NEL

*W*hat the hell is happening right now? Jake kissed me. Twice! I mean, what am I meant to do with that? He kissed me under the mistletoe last night and then gave me a completely platonic massage—if that's even a thing. He's flirting one minute and then drawing boundaries that keep me firmly in the *best friend's little sister* zone the next. I'm both letting my excitement soar and trying to talk it down from the ledge. Jake Partridge does not have deep feelings for me. He's obviously swept up in some Christmas fantasy and thinks a bit of holiday fun would make the weekend better. I can't go down that road or my heart would be shredded like the wrapping paper on all those boxes under Harry's tree, then thrown out with the rest of the recycling on Boxing Day. To Jake, I may be a fun distraction. But to me, he's always been the one guy no one could ever live up to.

After he kissed me—the second time—we didn't have time to discuss anything as we both realised we had to hustle to catch the 11:48 back to the Surrey suburb and Pear Street. So, rather than asking him a tonne of questions about what his lips on mine actually meant, we hauled-arse back to the tube. It was positively heaving on this delightful Christmas Eve, then we battled the crowds at Waterloo only to be packed in like sardines on the train. It's a bit difficult to talk about anything without twenty other people hearing it as we're crowded in the vestibule. I'm pushed up against the wall by the doors and Jake is plastered to

84

my front, his arms braced either side of my shoulders. In an empty room, it would be a compromising position. In a crowded train carriage, I get the overwhelming sense that Jake is being the buffer between me and the other bodies bumping and stumbling against each other. He's protecting me, throwing cold glares to anyone who knocks into him and subsequently me.

When we get into his car that he'd parked at the station, I think he's going to say something but then his phone rings; his mother calling from Australia. He's on the phone the whole way to Pear Street where the road has been cordoned off. We're able to park at the hotel and then start on foot to the Christmas Eve fair that's been set up. Lisa has been working with some kind of committee and the local school to organise the Christmas Eve fair where anyone from the local area can set up a stall. Then tonight—according to the all-important itinerary—we are attending a holiday party at the Old Orchard Village Hall. Mulled wine, Santa, and reindeer included.

The fair is nearly as packed as the city. Families in big puffy coats with bobble hats and fingerless gloves roam amongst makeshift stalls. Some look professional with gazebos overhead while others are just fold out tables with handwritten signs on A4 paper. There are crafts and baked goods and Christmas games and coffee stands. A river of people flows through the narrow street, streams meandering off to the little market stalls and the atmosphere is buzzing. The sounds of happy chatter and laughter mixes with a brass band playing carols somewhere in the distance. Honestly, it's kind of magical. You know, if you like people. Which I don't.

We stroll up the middle of the road and I'm surrounded by people. Surrounded. There are so many of them and most of them are taller than me so I can't see more than a few inches in front of me. I can feel panic rising in the pit of my stomach, the tendons in my shoulders tightening. The sounds, which from a safe distant were cheerful and spirited, are becoming too loud and shrill. I feel my footsteps slowing as my feet feel like lead. Too many people. Not enough room.

Before it has a chance to bubble and manifest into something, everything pauses and calms with the feeling of warm skin on mine. Jake's hand is wrapped around my fingers. When I look up at him, he's looking at me with knotted brows.

"You okay?"

"Yeah," I croak, trying not to sound pathetic and probably failing miserably. "Just not great with lots of people."

He doesn't roll his eyes or laugh; he nods once and goes from holding my hand to wrapping an arm around my shoulders. Keeping me close and directing me to the pavement behind the row of vendors where the flow of people is so much lighter, and breathing becomes easier. Placing me against the low wall separating someone's front garden to the path, he stands in front of me so people have to swerve around him and avoid me altogether.

"You need a minute?" he asks, looking down at me with those whiskey eyes.

"I'm fine," I say, a little shakily.

"We'll take a minute," he says seriously.

What is happening between us? The question is on the tip of my tongue and if I didn't have that annoying voice in my head—which often sounds uncannily like my brother—telling me that it would sound needy and pathetic to ask such a thing, I would just blurt it out. The decision is taken away from me by Rhiannon's voice calling to us.

"Jake! Nel!" She's walking up the pavement with Freddie on her hip. Luke is just behind her with Margot on his shoulders. They all smile at us, their cheeks rosy from the cold and their eyes bright in the strong sun. Both Jake and I wave at them as they approach.

"Hey guys, having fun?" Jake asks, pinching Freddie's little cheek.

"Yeah," Freddie shrieks with much enthusiasm.

"Have you two bumped into Lisa yet?" Rhiannon asks with a look of amusement.

"No, we just got here," Jake answers for us.

Rhiannon and Luke exchange a look. "Oh, well good luck when you do."

"Why?" I ask, frowning up at them from my perched position.

"Well, let's just say that everything seems to have been going wrong for her this morning. She may normally channel her inner Martha Stewart, but when her itinerary is messed with, she's more Annie Wilkes."

"Who?" I frown.

"Misery," Jake says, like that answers that. "Kathy Bates, psycho killer?"

I shake my head. No idea what they're talking about. "What's been going wrong?" I ask instead.

"Oh, she'll tell you all about it," Luke smirks.

"I don't like the mischief in your eyes, dude," Jake grumbles and pulls me up by my hand, lacing his fingers through mine. I don't miss the look of surprise on Rhiannon's face, and I flush in embarrassment. I'd be surprised to see Jake Partridge holding hands with someone like me too.

He pulls me along the quieter pathway for a little while, Rhiannon and her family veering off to see the offerings and be amongst the hustle and bustle.

"You feeling up to trying the parade?" Jake asks.

"Sure," I give a watered-down smile.

"I've got you," he says with a reassuring squeeze of my hand.
Yes, you certainly do.

In the thick of it, we walk past vendors and patrons, the band getting louder as we move further up the street. Jake pulls me to one side towards an older lady sat behind a fold out table littered with what must be at least fifty snow globes. There are big ones, small ones, bright ones, muted ones, and some with lights inside. Jake picks one up, smiling like a kid at…well, Christmas.

"Man, I used to get one of these every year for Christmas when I was a kid." He shakes the globe in his hand and watches with fascinated nostalgia as tiny white snowflakes and glitter flit and flutter around a snowman and a Christmas tree. "Didn't you used to love them?" he asks, turning to me.

"I don't think I ever had one." I wrack my brain trying to think.

"What?!"

"Sorry, guess we just weren't snow globe people," I shrug.

"Unacceptable. There's magic in a snow globe, you know?"

"Oh yeah?"

"Absolutely, you shake up a snow globe and you automatically get a little Christmas spirit. Like fairy dust has been sprinkled on you or something."

I snort a laugh. "You're a weird guy, Jake."

"Come on, we could all use a little Christmas spirit all year round."

I huff and feel a slight prickle at the back of my eye. "I don't feel like I have much Christmas spirit on Christmas Eve, let alone the rest of the year."

He looks at me, his shoulders sagging in sympathy. "The first year is going to be hard, Nel. I'm here if you need me."

"Thank you," I whisper, looking at the snow globes, and batting away tears with my lashes.

"And hey, you know your brother is going through it all too. You can also talk to him."

Tsk. "I'm pretty sure Harry is fine. He was straight into funeral planning and probate meetings; he doesn't need me to lean on. He doesn't need me at all. I just annoy him."

Jake hangs his head and shakes it in some sort of frustration. "You two are really something," he mumbles.

88

"Huh?"

"Nothing. Look, Harry needs you. You guys need each other. Trust me."

"Uh, okay." I nod, not truly believing him.

We walk for just a few minutes more before we run into Harry. Jake drops my hand immediately when my brother comes into view and although it's completely understandable, it stings.

"Everything go okay this morning?" Harry says as he hugs me hello. It throws me off for a second because I don't think he's ever asked me about work.

"Yeah, great," I say. But when he's pulling back, he doesn't look like he's listening. His eyes dart around as if looking for someone. Lucas and Oscar come running up to us and tug on their dad's coat.

"She's just over there," Oscar puffs, pointing a little way up the road to where I can see Lisa talking animatedly to another woman.

Harry turns to us with panic in his eyes. "Listen, do me a favour, yeah? Lisa is stressing a little today and I need you to agree to whatever she asks of you."

"What is she going to ask?" I question.

"Just promise me!" Harrys eyes bounce between Jake and me.

"Okay, dude. Chill a bit, yeah?" Jake grabs his shoulder and attempts to calm him.

Lisa is with us in a second—surprisingly quick given the bowling ball on her abdomen—and for the first time ever, she looks flustered with actual hairs out of place.

"Hi guys," she says, rather breathlessly.

"Hey Lis, how's it going?" Jake asks, putting his arm over her shoulders.

"Eurgh, awful. People keep letting me down. Seven people who said they were having stalls today have just not shown up, which means I have gaps!" She throws her hands up in

89

frustration. "The sanctuary bringing the reindeer tonight now say they're only bringing four, not eight like planned. Cheryl thought she was being so helpful buying the milk for the hot chocolate stand early but now it's all out of date, so we had send someone to get more. Then there's the biggest problem of all..."

"Which is?" Jake asks.

Lisa looks at him and then at me, pleading in her eyes. I get a sick sense that I'm about to be guilted into something I really don't want to do.

"Well, I need a favour."

CHAPTER FOURTEEN:
"Oh my God, you look ridiculous!"

JAKE

I teach teenagers. So I'm no stranger to making a prat of myself, *for the kids*. Which is why when Lisa asked me to do this, I was fine with it. I mean, I've done worse in the name of education. I once dressed as William Shakespeare and stood on a table to recite the famous *To be or not to be* speech in my best thespian voice, only for one kid to ask why I was dressed as Shakespeare when I should have been dressed as Hamlet. I told them my Hamlet costume was stuck at the dry cleaners and got a little titter from the group. Good enough for me.

This is different though, there is more of an audience and the kids will be smaller. I was the only one who could do it as I have a criminal background check for my job. When you're inviting little kids to sit on your lap, their parents feel more comfortable when they know you haven't been convicted of being a creeper. Nel however, is far less comfortable than I am with our game of dress-up. I've been ready in my red and white suit for about twenty minutes while she's been in the bathroom. The jacket is hanging off me as I don't have the physique for Santa, but Lisa says she will rectify that when we meet her at the hall, which sounds ominous.

"You okay in there?" I call through the closed door.

Silence.

"Nel? Can you just give me a sign that you're alive or something."

"I look ridiculous!" The desperation in her voice has me cracking a smile.

"I'm sure that's not true," I try to reassure.

"I *cannot* wear this in front of kids, I'll be arrested."

"Just come out, I'm sure it's fine," I chuckle.

The door bursts open and my humour dies. My knees buckle slightly as I sit on the edge of the bed looking at Nel. Ho-lee shit.

I recall her telling Lisa that the elf costume she'd handed her was not going to fit and Lisa confidently telling her it was stretchy and basically *one size fits all*. Nel had looked sceptical, and I understand why. It's not that it doesn't fit because I'd say it fits *perfectly*. However, it's not exactly what it looked like on the packet. The fabric is moulded to her every curve and stretched obscenely over her chest; the neckline is trimmed with white fluffy stuff that whisps over the pale flesh of her deep cleavage. The green felt of her dress only falls halfway down her thighs and her legs are covered by red and white candy cane tights—or maybe they're stockings. Oh God, let them be stockings. She wears black lace-up ankle boots with a chunky heel, and she has a hat that matches mine except hers is green where mine is red. She's done her makeup with green all around her eyes and red glittery lips, even managing a small red glittery heart under one eye. Her light brown hair is wavy and loose, falling below her breasts and it takes every bit of energy I have not to wrap it around my fist and make her tremble.

Things are weird. I keep kissing her and that's probably the wrong way to go about things. What is it they say? Communication is key. I should try that. I should tell her that I really want to take her out, that I think I've had feelings for her for years, and that I think she's the most beautiful woman in the world. Unfortunately though, when we're alone together, my dick seems to do the thinking. With the wrong brain running the show, I have been acting a little more caveman than I would normally, pawing at her like a crazed animal. Which is what I want to do right now, so I sit on my hands. It's the only way.

"See?" Nel gestures to herself, effectively breaking my thoughts. "Ridiculous!"

"You uh…you don't look ridiculous," I croak, trying to control my racing heart and growing cock.

"Jake," she reasons. "I can't go out like this. Look!" She turns to show me the back and I think a little drool slips from my mouth. Where the dress goes over her bum, it's a little shorter in the back and only just covers said posterior. Oh lord. The tiny glimpse of the top of her stockings seemingly attached to a garter has so much blood rushing south that I feel lightheaded. "If I bend over, even just a little bit," she continues, "I'll show the whole village my arse!"

"Care to demonstrate?"

She glares at me over her shoulder. "You're not helping."

"I think you look great," I say honestly.

"It's too short," she whines.

"At least it came with stockings." I try looking on the positive but that delicious blush rises on her cheeks.

"Actually, these were mine. And I need suspenders to keep them up so I had to wear that red thing you've been eyeing in my case as my only suspenders are attached to it."

I try not to let my jaw drop, but I fail. Let's move on. "And now I know what's underneath," I mumble almost to myself. My hand reaches out and my knuckle grazes the soft fabric of her skirt, a thoughtless act, instinctual really.

"Yeah, well one wrong move tonight and so will the rest of Pear Street," she huffs.

Old Orchard Village Hall is not like the old halls I knew as a child, all beige and squeaky floors, smelling of mothballs and old woman perfume. No, this one is sleek and modern with pine beams and solid wood flooring, distinctly lacking any creeks. It smells new, like fresh paint and wood. We arrive early so as not to ruin the illusion for all the kiddies, seeing me—a.k.a Santa— arriving in a Volkswagen.

There is the distinct sound of setting up with furniture scraping on the floor, orders being barked, and the clinking of metal that sounds like cutlery. When we walk into the main hall, Lisa totters over to us with a huge smile.

"Oh, you guys look amazing!" She pulls Nel into a hug. "I told you it would fit."

The face Nel gives her has me disguising my laugh with a cough. "I'm seriously concerned about flashing minors here, Lisa."

Lis gives her a thoughtful once over. "Just don't bend down, you'll be fine. Or you'll be giving some hyped up pre-teens some very confusing feelings to go to bed with tonight."

Nel's eyes widen in horror and I throw my head back laughing with my whole body.

"And you," Lisa points to me. "Your belly is not shaking like a bowl full of jelly. Let's rectify that." From a table behind us, she pulls some white fuzz like what they stuff teddy bears with and without any care for propriety, she undoes the belt around my waist.

"Ex-squeeze me! Buy a man dinner first!"

Her eyebrows raise at my bare chest. "Did you not wear a t-shirt underneath?"

"Clearly not, Lis." I cover my bare nipples with my hands.

"Oh baby boy," she shakes her head, trying to suppress her smirk. "You're going to regret that."

Passing me the stuffing, she walks away laughing and I stick my tongue out at her retreating back. Holding the fuzz over my abdomen, I wrap the jacket back round me and do the belt up. Immediately, I understand Lisa's amusement as the material feels like fire ants covered in itching powder over my skin. I'm about to tell Nel that I may have made a mistake but her eyes are downcast and her bottom lip rolling between her teeth.

"Hey, you okay?"

"Are you in love with Lisa?"

Excuse me while I just pick my jaw up off the floor.

"I mean, I get it," she keeps going when I'm unable to form sentences. "She's perfect. Like, Mummy Barbie or something." She sounds resigned and I'm utterly confused.

"Why the Hell would you think that?" I finally manage.

"You two have your own jokes and you're really close and, like I said, she's perfect. It would make sense."

I huff out a breath, trying to calm myself because honestly, I'm getting annoyed. How have my actions over the last couple of days made Nel think that I have eyes for *anyone* but her? "Lisa and I are close," I agree. "Because she's my best friend's wife, it makes sense that we both get along. We're both closest to the same person." I turn to Nel, finding her nodding at me but her face is still uncertain. "Lisa is perfect." I step over to her and drag her lip from her teeth with my thumb. "For Harry." She blinks up at me as I keep her jaw cradled in my palm. "But she doesn't hold a candle to y—"

"Oh my God, you look ridiculous!" Harry strides over, not even noticing that fact that I'm second away from kissing his sister *for the third time in two days.*

"You're one to talk," Nel says, stepping away from me and gesturing at his Christmas jumper. A red monstrosity with a 3D chimney wrapped in real LED fairy lights and Santa's legs hanging out the bottom.

He shrugs. "I lost a bet with Luke last night. The man can drink." He looks at Nel and barely contains the disapproval in his face before he turns to me. "Did I see my wife undressing you earlier? What was that about?"

"She has no boundaries," I say, by way of answer and he just nods.

"She gets a little crazy at these things. Good luck with that as you're basically her employees now." He claps me on the shoulder and walks away. *Dick.*

The hall looks good, there's a large tree in one corner and tinsel everywhere. I find myself looking for sneaky mistletoe, any excuse. But I come up short. Along one wall is a large buffet that's been laid out with sandwiches, sausage rolls, and miniature cakes, among other things. But it's the cakes I have my eye on. Just getting into character, you know?

In the far corner is the Santa's grotto, made from carboard by the look of it, surrounded by fake snow and what can only be described as a throne next to it. That's where we head as I pull my fake beard from where I'd stuffed it in my pocket, position it on my face, and take my pew. Nel stands awkwardly to one side, fidgeting and tugging at the hem of her skirt.

"You nervous, little elf?"

Her eyes widen slightly before shrugging it off. "I'm not great with kids," she admits.

"You seem okay with Lucas and Oscar."

"I feel steam-rolled by Lucas most of the time. Oscar is quieter than most kids and I can think around him. But children in general are exhausting and loud and chaotic and I just can't do it for long periods. I guess that makes me a terrible Aunt."

I look at her for a long second and see the genuine insecurity in her eyes. "You are *not* a terrible Aunt. Those boys love you. So, you aren't in any hurry to have any of your own?"

She pulls a face like I'd just asked her if she wanted a jam and pickle sandwich. "There will be *no* children in my future."

I smirk at her determination. "Mine neither."

"What?" She snaps her head to me, her face incredulous.

"I don't want children," I shrug.

"How can that be? You're *so* good with kids, you're like super Uncle to the boys, even the twins adore you and they hardly know you. You're a teacher! You love kids!" The passion she has for the topic is really quite funny.

"I *do* love children. Kids are funny and curious and blunt, and they're our future. But they're also a lot of hard work and a lot of emotional ups and downs. The best thing about being Super-Uncle and a teacher is that at the end of the day, I get to give them back."

She chuckles. "Well, that makes me feel better. Most people think I'm some wicked villain for not wanting kids. But if a perfect human being like you doesn't want them, I guess I can't be so bad."

I frown at her, ticking over what she said. "You're a little obsessed with '*perfect,*'" I note, using air quotes.

She hangs her head. "I'm not normally. I guess just being around Harry and Lisa and you makes me feel ever so *imperfect*."

Well, I don't like that. Not one bit. "I've already told you. You're perfect, to me at least."

CHAPTER FIFTEEN
"It's like trying to enjoy your favourite chocolate bar whilst cleaning your teeth."

NEL

Jake is right. Kids are curious. I have had to make up a lot of answers to unexpected questions in a very short time. For example, did you know that when there is no chimney on a house, Santa enters from the drainage and pops out the toilet? Yeah, well neither did I until I sprouted that little fact from the panicked recesses of my brain.

There are loads of them, children I mean. Every household from The Old Orchard must have children under thirteen. The line to sit on '*Santa's*' lap was nearly out the door at one point. Of course, out the door are four fluffy reindeer that the kids are more than happy to fawn over. Luckily, the queue has subsided so Jake and I have a moment of respite. The hall is loud with the symphony of merriment and festivities. Couples seem to be more affectionate in the holiday spirit, which may have something to do with the strong holiday spirit in the spiked hot chocolate. Harry bought both Jake and I one of those tasty treats, mine with salted caramel Bailey's and his with peppermint liqueur, because he is apparently an animal.

"What's wrong with peppermint?" he asks defensively when I turn my nose up.

"Whoever thought that it should go with chocolate was not right in the head. It's like trying to enjoy your favourite chocolate bar whilst cleaning your teeth."

"Riiiight," he drawls. "But putting salt in caramel was a perfectly normal thing to do?"

"Everyone knows it brings out the sweetness." I scowl at him over the rim of my paper cup. "Savour that, Santa. No one wants a sloppy Chris Cringle."

"Sloppy Chris Cringle indeed," he scoffs, taking a dainty sip from his own cup with his pinkie sticking out. I can't help but laugh.

My giggle is cut off with a yelp when I feel a sharp pinch on my bottom. Spinning around, I'm horrified to find a young boy grinning up at me, he must be no more that twelve and smells strongly of that cheap body spray that teenage boys seem to like to bathe in. It reminds me of school discos. I'm too shocked to find words.

"Hey!" Jake barks and the kid runs away. "Are you okay?" he asks me.

"Of course, just surprised," I say, rubbing my sore cheek.

"One minute." He walks away, approaching a couple in the crowd. The young boy is hiding behind the man's legs.

I watch as Father Christmas talks to, who I'm assuming to be the boy's parents, speaking low and looking very serious. Quite a feat considering he's wearing a fake beard and teddy bear stuffing. They all look over to me and the mother makes an audible gasp, turning to her son and raging at him through clenched teeth. I can only watch it all unfold with my brows practically tucked under my hairline. Then, to my utter horror, they all approach, the boy being dragged by his upper arm by his father.

"What do you say to the lady, Scott?" the father growls.

Scott was not happy to be stood in front of me. His face practically turns in on itself and he only grunts at me until his mother flicks his ear. "I'm sorry, Miss.," he mumbles at the ground.

"We are so sorry," the mother says with genuine regret.

"No worries," I manage through my mortification.

The family steps away as Santa resumes his throne.

"I can't believe you told on him." I shake my head.

"If boys are not held responsible for their actions when they're young, they grow up to be self-serving, arrogant, little pricks."

"That's what you teach in class, is it? Don't grow up to be a self-serving, arrogant, little prick?" I smirk over my shoulder at him, spying him slouched in the chair, legs spread wide. Even in the suit, the stuffing, and the fake beard, I'm a little turned on. *What is wrong with me?*

"Too right," he grins. "That and don't be a whiny lil' bitch," he stage-whispers to avoid offending tiny ears.

"Yes, *sir*." I don't know why my body dips in a little half-curtsey with my teasing, but Jake's humour fades and he raises a brow with a fire burning in his eyes, sending heat between my legs. Damn.

Before long, the queue to meet Santa is building again so we dutifully bring the children forward one-by-one. I listen in as Jake puts on an overly deep voice, throwing in the occasional '*ho ho ho.*' The kids love him—who wouldn't? Sooner rather than later we have seen all the children and Lisa allows us to step away from the grotto but laughs when we tell her we haven't brought a change of clothes.

So we mingle as Santa and his elf. Jake is getting antsy, fidgeting and shifting from one foot to the other. I notice him plucking at the fake bulge on his abdomen and every so often, Lisa bats his hand away. Poor thing must be getting uncomfortable with his added insulation. For some reason, I find it highly amusing.

We're split up as Jake is dragged to play with Lucas and Oscar, while Cami and Hen want to introduce me to a group of ladies they've been telling everything about me and my photography. I think they're trying to drum up business for me and it feels impolite to tell them that I'm fully booked for six months. Making polite conversation, my eyes keep drifting to Jake and every time, I catch him looking at me. That kiss is playing on my mind, and I want that conversation over with. I want to be out of this purgatory of not knowing what is happening between us. I also want to kiss him again. Judging by the look he's giving me, he's thinking a similar thing.

Unspoken agreements seem to be made and we make our excuses. To be honest, this little soirée is quite fun, and I would be happy to stay a while, which is quite unlike me. It seems navigating social functions is so much easier with the watchful eye of Jake Partridge on me. Nonetheless, I have a distinct feeling the hotel is where I want to be right now.

CHAPTER SIXTEEN
"Are you ticklish, little elf?"

NEL

"**O**h my god. Open the fucking door, Forrest, or I'm going to strip in the hallway."

"I'm trying!" I giggle as the electronic lock flashes red once more. I think my laughter is hindering my ability right now and I'll admit that the thought of Jake getting naked in the corridor is not making me go any faster.

"Try harder," he snarls in my ear. It's all in jest but that gravelly rasp blowing air over the back of my ear, hitting that sweet spot just below the lobe makes me shiver and my giggles subside. Finally, the door flashes green and I push it open. Jake barrels in and stops at the foot of the bed, he practically rips the belt off. Tearing open the jacket, he frantically pushes the white, synthetic stuffing away from his skin and I watch in fascinated amusement as I click the door closed and lean back on it.

Soon, he's stood there in his heavy boots, red trousers cuffed in white fur now sitting low enough on his hips that the waistband of his black Calvin Klein's is showing, an oversized Santa jacket open wide, and a Santa hat. His chest is heaving from his desperation to remove the offending stuffing and the moonlight being the only light in the room shines on his slightly sweaty skin. His torso is slightly pink from where it has been irritated, and fuck me if that doesn't make him hotter. For the love of Christmas, he looks good. *Do I have a Santa kink now?*

I swallow hard as my mouth floods and I dart my tongue out to wet my lips, my eyes locking with his. *Yep, not a Santa kink, definitely just a Jake kink.* Our easy joking from mere seconds ago fizzles and dies, making way for something more. Something darker. Jake's brow seems heavier as he looks at me, his eyes blatantly roving over me from my face to my toes, and I'm acutely aware of my ridiculous get up. Although it's not seeming so ridiculous now. I clutch the hem of my little green dress and hitch it ever so slightly up my thigh, just enough to show where my candy cane stockings are attached to the cherry-red suspenders. What am I doing? Why would I set myself up for such a disappointment? It's because I want to get a reaction from him. To know once and for all if it would be interest or disgust. My question is answered immediately when his eyes flash white hot. Lust.

Time stands still as we stare at each other. Neither of us know what to do. Should he head to the bathroom and change, leaving this tension to ease away? Should I stop staring at his bare chest like I want to lick it? *Who knows?* As it turns out, we do neither of those things. Instead, I choose to lean into the moment, pressing my shoulders into the door and lifting my hips slightly, continuing to ease my skirt up my legs until my red, lace panties are on show. My heart is thundering in my chest, my nerves almost making me stop and cover myself again, but Jake swallows and his fingers twitch by his thigh like he wants to touch me. I don't really know where to go from here. If I were more confident, I'd slip my hands into my underwear and rub myself while he watches. But I'm nowhere near that bold. This isn't a carefully posed photograph that I can re-take over and over until I'm happy with it before it's shown to an audience. This is happening for real, and I can't guarantee I'll look good; I can't even see myself. Doubt is starting to creep in and I'm just about to lower my dress when Jake interrupts the fog of uncertainty.

"Come here." Low and commanding, his voice drapes me in a momentary calm. Pushing off from the door, I walk over to him in slow, slightly shaky strides. When I'm stood in front of him, he places one hand on my waist and I can't help the slight flinch. I don't like people feeling the soft rolls of my body but when I

103

don't see any reaction other than that same burning desire in his eyes, I relax into him. He steps forward, closing what little gap there is between us until I have to arch my neck to look up at him. "What are you doing, little elf?"

Oh God, do I have to say it? "What do you mean?"

The growl that leaves his throat is feral and it hits me right between the legs. "Don't play dumb, Nel. What are you trying to start here?" His face dips, just enough that I can feel his breath wisping across my lips with each word. My breasts are pressed to his ribs, the steady movement of his heavy breaths rubs my nipples through the fabric of my dress.

"I-I'm not sure."

His other hand slowly comes up to gently cup my jaw and I'm aware of my breath coming out heavy. It must be hitting his lips with how closely he is hovering over me. "Tell me what you want, Nel. If you don't tell me, I can't give it to you."

I want you to fuck me, suck on my nipples and squeeze my arse. *Yeah, I can't say that.* Saying that out loud gives him the chance to laugh in my face and call me a silly kid. "I want…"

His eyes widen in anticipation, his tongue slowly tracing his bottom lip and I inch forward until there is barely a hair's breadth between us.

"I want…" I try again. But I can't say exactly what I want. Instead, I give him a slow and practiced seductive smile. "I want you to keep the hat on."

His eyes dart right to where the white fluffy pom-pom is dangling by his cheek, and he tosses his head back and laughs. My smile stretches until my cheeks ache, his laugh is so deep and throaty, the sound reverberates through me from where my chest rubs against his. "Okay, Forrest. I'll keep the hat on if you tell me what I'll be doing while wearing it."

"You're really going to make me say it?" I grumble.

"Oh yeah, I'm really going to make you say it. For two reasons."

"Which are?" I move without thinking, my fingertips trailing up his sides, feeling his hot skin tremble beneath my touch.

"One, because I want to be completely clear on what you want; I would hate to misinterpret things."

"Hmm," I hum into his touch as he slides his hand from my jaw into my hair at the nape of my neck.

"And two, because I want to hear those words from your sweet lips."

I can't bring myself to say what I really want, so for now I settle on, "Kiss me."

He doesn't seem to mind the PG-13 request; he leans down to close the last two inches between us. And just like that, I'm kissing Jake Freakin' Partridge. *Again.* In a mid-range hotel on Pear Street. His lips are deceptively soft as he brushes them over mine, his hand at my waist tightening, pulling me further into his embrace. The hand in my hair holds me in place so he can kiss me how he wants. I'm suddenly desperate for him to deepen the kiss, to touch me everywhere, and take this as far as it can go. But when I arch into him and try to take more, he holds me steady and smiles against my mouth.

"Tell me what you need, little elf." His lips are still on mine, so I can feel them move with each word and taste the peppermint candy cane on his breath.

My skin is crawling with need by this point, there's a throbbing between my legs and I feel empty. Fuck it. We're doing this. "I need you, Jake. I need you to touch me. I need your mouth, your hands, and most importantly I need your cock, and I need it now."

He blinks at me for a moment and for half a second, I worry that I have vastly misread the situation but then he closes his eyes and rests his forehead on mine, still holding me close to his body. "That is so fucking hot."

"I also need to come. You up for the challenge, Santa?" I raise a brow at him, daring him to accept.

105

He rumbles from his chest and attacks my mouth with his again. This time it's not gentle, teasing strokes. He ravages me with firm lips and a plundering tongue. I whimper into his kiss, running my hands up his sides to his shoulder blades, feeling the strong muscles of his back flex and move as his hands roam over my body. For the first time ever, I don't feel self-conscious. Maybe it's the way Jake is so firm and sure with his touch, not hesitant or curious. He touches me like he already knows what he will find and already loves it, like he's too eager to feel every inch of me. It's a heady feeling to be craved, and I am here for it.

I slide his jacket from his shoulders, down his arms and break away from Jake's lips to look down at him. He's so...big. Every inch is packed with muscle, his pecs are firm under my touch, his light tan even across his skin. His abdomen tight with a clearly defined six-pack and sharp vee at his hips, pointing to what I really want under his red felt trousers. Jake's delicious muscles tremble as I rake my festive nails over his stomach and hook my finger in his waistband. My voice comes out as a whisper when I finally give him what he wants. "Fuck me, Jake."

He wastes no time. Crashing his lips to mine, he holds my face in both of his rough hands. Dipping my fingers under the waist of his pants, I don't go where he probably wants me, choosing instead to reach round to squeeze his peachy butt, digging my nails into his flesh and pulling him close to me.

"Please, Nel," he begs against my lips, the plea sounding almost pained.

"Please what?" I breathe, genuinely not knowing what he needs because my brain has turned to cotton candy.

"Let me see." When I pull away and just frown at him, not understanding, because—like I said—there is nothing but sweet fluff inside my skull, he clarifies, "Take off your dress, let me see what's underneath."

Oooooh. Yeah, forgot about that for a second. So here's the thing, I can wear the hell out of a lingerie set, I know I can. I have practiced the art of modelling sets like this a lot and I know my photos look great. But it's been a while since I've actually been in front of someone in the flesh wearing so little. So, I'm a little hesitant when I take the hem of my dress in hand, gripping my bottom lip between my teeth.

"Nel, *please*. I'm dying here." I believe him, his expression begging, starved puppy-dog eyes and all. His pure desperation is an aphrodisiac, sending confidence through my nerves and making me feel sexy.

I pull the dress up and over my head, knocking my little green hat to the floor in the process. Jake's eyelids droop slightly like the sight of me is drugging, and every inch of me that he takes in gets him higher. The set I'm wearing is beautiful. The candy cane stockings are held up by suspenders attached to a cherry red satin belt that sits on my waist and is shaped with short rods of boning. The knickers are alternating panels of lace and silk in a boy-short style. The bra has plunging satin cups trimmed in lace, and a lace body that extends a couple of inches below my breasts so there is only an inch of skin on show between it and the belt. The bra fastens at the front with a row of hooks and eyes running between my breasts.

"Oh, holy night," Jake whispers and I chuckle as heat floods my cheeks. He sits on the end of the bed and just stares at me. I can see his jaw is tight even under his short beard, his Adam's apple dips on a hard swallow. "You are perfect."

I don't know how to respond to that. No one has ever told me I was perfect before Jake, and he's told me twice today. "It's the lingerie, it could make anyone look good."

For the first time since my dress came off, he looks me in the eye, his face serious as he shakes his head in disagreement. When his hand reaches out to touch me, I pull back slightly.

"Don't damage it," I warn, one finger held up in caution. "I still have to take photos to post or I have to pay the two hundred quid for it."

He smirks, the pompom from his Santa hat sitting at the edge of his smile. "Why would I ruin something so beautiful, little elf?" Grabbing my waist, he yanks me forward, tearing a gasp from me. When I'm stood between his spread legs, he runs light fingers up the back of my thighs, tracing the edge of my stockings. His head dips forward, running his nose between my breasts and I place my palms on his bare shoulders, trying to slow my racing heart with slow and steady breaths.

"Mmmm," he rumbles. "You smell so good."

"And you taste of mint chocolate," I smirk down on him.

"We all have our flaws," he smiles against my breast before closing his mouth over my nipple through the soft satin. My head falls back on a moan as the wet heat seeps through the fabric and his tongue probes around the pebbled flesh. Sliding my hand to the back of his head, I hold him there as my pulse throbs between my legs, causing me to squirm.

"Jake," I pant. He pops off my breast and observes the dark, wet patch he left behind. His hands come to my hips and one finger trails below the line of the suspender-belt, where my stomach overhangs. I can feel myself tense, not liking how intimately he's getting to know my fupa. I wonder briefly if he's ever been with someone bigger, then push the thought away as it ignites some very unpleasant emotions that should not be at the forefront right now.

"What just happened?" I look down to see Jake looking at me with furrowed brows and concern in his eyes.

"Wh-what do you mean?"

"You tensed. Are you okay?"

I swallow, feeling strangely emotional because, you know, this is Jake and I'm...me. *Perfect*. That's what he said, but I'm having a hard time feeling it. Because I feel that honesty is the best policy, I tell him, "I don't want to disappoint you."

"Oh, little elf," he says, shaking his head, before gripping me at the back of my knees until my legs give way. I fall to the bed and Jake leans back so I land on top of him, my legs straddling his narrow hips. "You are everything I've been fantasising about; how could you ever disappoint me?"

He pulls my head to his for a scorching kiss, his other hand roaming down my body to take a palmful of my arse and pulling me down, encouraging me to grind against the growing length in his pants. I'm wetter than a summer slip 'n' slide and desperate for something, something *more*. Jake is in no rush though, rolling us so I'm on my back, kissing down my neck, chest, ribs, and stomach. Each press of his lips sends a buzz through my veins and a pulse to my pussy.

He slowly stands at the end of the bed taking my calf in his hands and bringing my booted foot to rest on his bare chest. With slow and measured movements, he pulls at my laces, untying my boot and pulling it from my foot before repeating the routine with my other leg. With both my feet on his pecs, he runs his hands over my shins, to my ankles, and up over the top of my feet to my toes. On the way back, he drags his thumbnail over my instep and I automatically jerk away and squeal. His eyebrow raises and his mouth stretches to a wicked smile.

"Are you ticklish, little elf?" He grabs for me again, but I squirm and wriggle to avoid his hands, laughing through my protests. "Oh, that is useful to know." He climbs over me, capturing my lips once more and sliding his tongue against mine. His beard is rough yet soft against my skin, his body weight feels delicious on top of me. "Right now, though," he murmurs against my lips, "I'm not interested in making you laugh." His hand runs down the side of my body, dipping into the waistband of my knickers until his long, strong fingers reach my centre. "Only in making you come."

CHAPTER SEVENTEEN
"Won't stop, can't stop."

JAKE

S o, talking is going very well. I honestly had every intention of getting back to the hotel to have the conversation that Nel and I needed. You know, the one about taking her out on a date, telling her I really like her, and that I'm interested in more than coming at her like a wild animal during mating season? But then I had to get rid of that God forsaken fake belly, and the way she looked at my naked chest made *me* feel like the hunted. When she started playing with the hem of her dress, teasing me with glimpses of that harlot red set, everything went a bit hazy. Hazy but focussed because everything that wasn't Nel wobbled like a 90s sitcom transitioning into a dream sequence. But Nel shone in ultra-definition and all conversation left my mind.

Nel is soft and pliant beneath me, her lips moving languidly against mine as she sucks gently on my tongue. No one has ever sucked on my tongue before and I can honestly say it's amazing and, if you have never tried it, you definitely should. My hand is completely in her underwear and my finger lightly traces her seam, not applying nearly enough pressure to ease her need, but teasing. When I do the same again, she groans in frustration, making me smile into her mouth.

"So needy, little elf."

"Jake," she whines. "I need more."

"Do you think you deserve more?" I ask, grinding my impossibly thick cock against her thigh. "Tell me, have you been a good girl, Nel?"

She bats thick eyelashes at me, smirking through an attempt at innocence. "Yes, Santa."

My hips jerk without volition and I press my finger between her folds to tease at her entrance while my thumb rolls circles around her clit. "You are so wet."

"It's what you do to me," she rasps, arching her back as I enter her with my middle finger.

"Is that so?" I suck lightly on the delicate skin of her neck above her pulse. When a second finger joins the first, I start to slowly pump them in and out of her.

"Yeah," she breathes, rolling her hips to fuck herself on my fingers.

The wet sounds are making my dick hard enough to almost punch through my boxers and the flimsy red trousers. But right now, nothing matters more than making her come for me.

"Pull your bra down," I demand, my voice a little more desperate than intended. She grips the satin cup of her bra and pulls it so her breast is exposed and pushed up, one perfectly pink nipple there for the taking. And take I do. I dip my head to pull that rosy bud into my mouth and suck hard on her sensitive flesh. She whimpers, arching her back to give me better access as I add a third finger inside her pussy and curl them to stroke at the sensitive spot of her inner walls.

"Jake...I...I'm gonna..."

I moan with her gorgeous tit still in my mouth, sucking hard enough to be slightly painful and flick my tongue over the hardened tip. Nel wails, a hand clamping onto the hair at the back of my head and her sweet cunt tightening around my fingers. I let go of her abused nipple and kiss her senseless as she soaks my hand.

"You're so goddamn beautiful," I tell her around my kisses and she whimpers in response. I'm not usually a hurried or selfish lover but I'm at breaking point right about now and I need inside her. Leaning over, I open the drawer of the small nightstand and pull out the box I'd placed there earlier.

She raises a brow at me and gives me a look of amused suspicion, one that I've been seeing more and more of, one that belongs to the new Nel. "You have condoms? Were you expecting to get laid this Christmas?"

I chuckle, sitting back on my heels and working the box with shaking hands. "No, but I thought I better take precautions after you've been jumping me every chance you get."

"*Me?!*"

I laugh again as she props herself up on her elbows to glare at me incredulously. "I didn't dare hope that I would get to be with you like this while we're here. But I knew that if the chance did arise, I certainly didn't want to be caught short. Which is why when you and Lisa were discussing elf costumes, I ducked into the pharmacy."

I get a foil packet out and start tearing it open, but she stops me. "Wait."

A moment of panic hits me, thinking she has changed her mind, but it soon falls away as she pulls at the waistband of my Santa pants and frees my desperate cock. She lightly scrapes the length of me with a pretty red nail and little Jake jumps in excitement. I'm not sure that the sound that comes out of me is entirely human when she wraps her fist around the base and gives me a firm, slow pull.

"I just want to feel you properly before you suit up," she murmurs, her eyes fixated on the swollen head of my dick.

"You better stop, little elf, or I'm not going to last." My voice is strained, and I can only look to the ceiling because the sight of her jerking me off is too much. I'm relieved when her hand leaves me but then a groan is ripped from my throat as wet heat surrounds my flesh. Looking down, I watch as Nel's light brown, wavy hair bobs up and down my length. Like she couldn't be any more perfect. Her fist twists at my base while her mouth focusses

112

on the crown and most of my length, sucking and humming, igniting flames on my skin. "Nel, you gotta stop, baby."

She lets go with a pop and looks up at me through thick lashes as she licks her lips. It's a little tricky getting the condom on with trembling fingers but my anticipation seems to be getting the better of me. Once I'm fully sheathed, I take those juicy lips with mine and lean over, forcing Nel to her back.

"You know," she mumbles against me. "It takes a little work to get these knickers off with the suspenders and everything."

"Who says you're taking them off?"

She raises that sexy brow at me again. "I told you, you can't destroy this set, Partridge."

I smile at her and it seems to do something to her as she bites her lip and squirms beneath me. "I won't. Trust me, little elf, this pretty thing will get further use yet."

When I slip my fingers in the hem of her red panties at her crotch and tug them to one side, she gasps. Whether it's from shock or concern for the state of her underwear, I can't quite say but I swallow the sound with my mouth on hers. My fingers glide along her slit with ease, lubricated by her earlier orgasm. When I'm satisfied she's wet enough for me, I position my cock at her entrance.

"You good, little elf?"

She nods and I push inside. "Oh, Jesus," she gasps.

"He's not here right now, just me, baby." I take myself as far as I can go, until my hips are flush to hers, then look down to see where we're joined. An expanse of red lace and satin, one leg clad in red and white stockings is hooked over my hip, my Santa pants are still halfway down my arse, and I realise in this moment that I still have my black boots on. But I'm not stopping for anything.

I start moving slowly and deliberately, bringing myself out of her welcoming heat to the tip before plunging back in. My weight rests on one elbow, the hand of which cradles to top of her head, protecting her from hitting the headboard, the other hand can't stop exploring her body. Her thick thighs flex in my hand as she rolls her hips against me, her soft belly feels amazing against my palm, her breast—too big to be contained in one of my hands—squeezes beautifully and the sounds she makes have my hips picking up pace.

"You're so beautiful." I can't help the praise falling from my lips onto hers. "You feel like heaven. You take my cock like a fucking dream, Nel."

"Jake," she gasps, locking her heels at the small of my back, the shift in position has me sinking deeper and we both groan into each other. "Jake, I'm close. Keep going, please," she sobs.

"Won't stop, can't stop," I chant. Sweat is pouring down my back and the different textures of her lingerie chafe deliciously against my bare skin. The hem of her panties that I pulled to one side, tickles along my length with each thrust and before I know it, I'm on the precipice. "I need you to come, baby."

"I'm close," she cries.

Every muscle in my body is tense with trying to hold off my own release. "Tell me what you need," I grind out through clenched teeth.

She seems to hesitate slightly, like she's afraid to ask for what she wants. Her kissed bruised lips roll inward, and her chocolate brown eyes widen.

"Baby, please," I beg her.

"Suck my nipple," she whispers.

Fuck yes. I can do that. I lower my mouth and take the hardened bud lightly between my teeth, sliding my tongue over the tip before taking as much of her breast in my mouth as possible. She groans a guttural, pleasured sound that pushes me over the edge. Nel's walls close around me like a fist as she comes and I slam inside her once more, pulling off her breast, before stilling inside her, letting myself fill the condom. I'm panting like I just ran a marathon and my body is tingling with

114

sweat, my head suddenly feels too heavy so it dips forward and Nel giggles. I look up to see that the ridiculous white pom-pom from my hat that I kept on—as requested—is lying on her cheek. I move my head so it glides over her face, and she laughs. The action has her clenching around my sensitive cock and I groan. Slipping out of her, I roll to my back next to her and stare up at the ceiling.

"You look ridiculous, definitely a sloppy Chris Cringle," she giggles. I look down at the red trousers halfway down my thighs, my boots still on, my chest bare, and the red hat still on my head. I turn to her and see a Christmas Angel. Her wavy hair is a halo around her head on the pillow, sex mussed and shining. She's still in that cherry red lingerie but one breast exposed, her nipple dark from my abuse and teeth marks indented in the soft flesh. Her underwear is still askew, a peek of dark brown curls poking through. Next time, I'm going to bury my face in those curls. I feel like I'm on top of the world. Turns out, fucking my best friend's little sister was the Christmas present I didn't know I wanted.

"And you look perfect, little elf."

CHAPTER EIGHTEEN
"Facial hair and hanging fruit don't really do it for me."

NEL

I wake up wrapped in Jake Partridge. And not for the first time this week. But today is different because today I wake up wrapped in Jake Partridge after he boned my brains out last night. Me, Nel Forrest. The quiet fat kid who used to stay behind after school to secretly watch his rugby practices from the art room window. When we'd finally caught our breath last night, he de-Santa-fied completely and I changed out of what will now forever be my favourite lingerie set—in the privacy of the bathroom because, hello, we're not at the letting-him-see-me-completely-naked stage yet—to get into bed, and each other's arms. Despite never wanting to share my bed with anyone, I have spent the entire night snuggled into Jake's warmth.

Now, my back is pressed firmly against his chest and his dick is rock hard against my arse. There's a niggling terror in the back of my mind that says he is going to wake up to regret last night. That the rush of lust was due to being drunk on peppermint hot chocolate and he'll think it better to never mention it again. *Damn, I really need to pee.* I give a testing wiggle to see how strong his hold is, and his arms clamp tighter around me, his hips grinding into me as he buries his face further into my hair. A shower of relief tamps down the flames of worry that were licking at my sub-conscious. He can't be too regretful if he is trying to get closer to me. Any closer and he'd be inside me again, but that is *not* happening until I pee.

116

"If you don't stop wriggling about, little Jake is going to bust a nut," he mumbles against my scalp.

"Oh my God," I laugh—not helping the whole bladder issue. "*Little* Jake? *Seriously?* That is *so* cringey, Jake."

"What do you want me to name him? *Brad*?"

"Do you have to name *it* at all?"

"He's my buddy," he says defensively.

"You're ridiculous." I try freeing myself again, but he just holds me to him.

"Why are you trying to escape me, woman? It's still the middle of the night."

I'll admit it's still dark out, but my bodily functions do not change with the shorter days. "I've got to use the bathroom!"

He grunts, "Fine, but I want your butt back in this bed and snuggling into little Jake again in less than three minutes."

I'm finally free and laugh all the way to the bathroom. I finish my business and wash my hands, wincing at the sight of myself in the mirror. I didn't take my makeup off last night and I'm a little smudged. I take a hair tie I'd left on the counter and get my hair out of my face so I can wash up a little. By the time I have cleared the green smudges above my eyes and the black ones below, Jake is snoring softly again. I tap my phone screen to see it's just gone seven and as we don't have to be at Harry's until after nine, I'm happy to luxuriate in my present circumstances for a moment or two.

Jake is truly a beautiful man. His dark brown hair is long enough to look mussed and thoroughly sexed; his whiskey brown eyes are closed so his enviously thick lashes fan against his high cheekbones. The dark scruff around his cheeks and jaw is a little longer than usual and in need of a good trim, but it still frames perfectly pink lips with a beautifully formed Cupid's bow. Then there's his body. This boy works *out*. I know he still plays rugby with Harry on weekends, but I'd say more work goes into the sculptured muscle of his chest and abdomen. The sheet covers him below his hips but I know they cover thick thighs and calves with course dark hair that feels amazing against my skin.

"Are you watching me sleep, Forrest?" he mumbles against his pillow without opening his eyes.

"No," I lie. "That would be creepy."

"Very creepy," he agrees. "Come back to bed, little elf."

I climb under the duvet and slide my body against his. He finally opens his eyes and looks down at me with a sleepy smile. "Hi," I whisper.

"Hello."

I want to know. I have to ask. "Jake?"

"Hm?" He pulls me closer, looking to be settling back in to sleep.

"What happens next?"

He looks down at me in question. "We go back to sleep for an hour and then get ready to join the rest for a jolly Christmas celebration."

"And after that?" I hate how uncertain my voice sounds.

He smiles wide at me and brushes some hair from my face. "Well, after Christmas, I have to go home as I'm on call with the fire station and working all over New Year."

"Right," I say, everything deflating.

"Then," he continues, cupping my jaw and holding me in position to maintain eye contact. "In the new year, I'm taking you to dinner."

My heart may have burst. *That's a bit sad, isn't it?* "Really?"

"Oh, yes. I'm talking fancy shit; flowers on the table, low lighting, real silverware. The works. You reckon there's somewhere like that in your town?"

"Are you asking if there are decent restaurants in London?"

"Mmm," he hums thoughtfully,

I snort...like a piggy. "Yes, I'm sure the capital has one or two nice places."

"Well then that settles it, I shall take you out in London." He trails his fingers up and down my bare arm as I rest my head on his chest, hearing the rhythmic beating of his heart.

"What about Harry?" I ask, tracing circles around his nipple.

"I mean, I *could* invite him but honestly, I think having your brother on our first date would make things a little awkward."

"You know what I mean," I giggle.

He chuckles and kisses the top of my head. "We can handle Harry however you want, baby. But just so you know, your brother has no say in who I do or do not sleep with. And he sure as Hell doesn't have a say in who you get to sleep with."

"I know that. I just don't want to," I hesitate, "disappoint him."

"Why do you think this would disappoint him?" he questions, not sounding hurt, just curious.

"Because I *always* disappoint him."

"That's not true."

"Still, I think maybe it's best that we don't say anything right now."

"Sure thing, little elf." He kisses my hair again. "We should probably get up."

"Probably," I groan.

"But first," he rolls so I'm on my back and he is on top of me. "Breakfast."

He plants a quick kiss on my lips before moving down my body, pulling my shorts down my legs and discarding them. Anticipation coils in my belly as I feel his hot breaths against my centre. He plants a wet, open-mouthed kiss to my pussy. The moment he touches me, my veins fill with fire and my uterus skips a beat. Using his thumbs, he parts my folds and delicately traces his tongue around my entrance, up to my clit but doesn't touch the sensitive nub, choosing to tease me by circling the area I want his attention.

119

"Jake," I whine, sliding my fingers into his thick hair and pressing him further into me.

I can feel his chuckle against me and it has me wiggling needily. "Oh, little elf, you're so easy to tease."

"I don't want to be teased," I complain, grinding myself against his beard and *oh sweet figgy pudding* that feels good.

He grabs my hips with bruising force, stilling me and unwanted self-consciousness hits me right in the chest as his fingers dig into too much flesh. I do not have visible hip bones even in a lying down position. "Patience, Nel." He smirks up at me over my belly from between my legs before frowning at whatever he sees on my face. "What's wrong?"

"Nothing," I say quickly, looking up to the ceiling so he can no longer read my face.

But he's not giving up. "Nel, what's wrong?"

"I'm sorry I don't have a great body like you." My cheeks are on fire, tears burning at the back of my eyes and I hate myself for it. I've worked hard to embrace and love the body I have; I was confident enough with my last boyfriend, but Jake has been the epitome of perfection in my mind for so long that I'm certain I don't stack up.

"You don't have a what?" He rears back like I've just said something offensive.

"Oh, God," I moan, covering my face with my hands. I have just ruined what was promising to be a very good moment.

I feel the bed dip and move as he climbs back over me and he uses his face to nudge my hands away. As soon as he has access, he claims my mouth, kissing me with slow and deliberate movements. The baseball bat in his boxers grinds against my bare pussy, making me forget my own thoughts.

"What in the ever-loving fuck made you think that I wasn't completely in awe of your body?"

"I don't look like you," I say lamely.

His smile makes me blush again. "Well, that's a good thing, because facial hair and hanging fruit don't really do it for me."

I try to glare at him but my mouth quirks up involuntarily. "You know what I mean."

"No, I don't. Explain it to me, Nel."

"Eurgh, Jake. Come on, don't make me say it." He just stares at me expectantly. "How many girls have you been with who need the seatbelt extender on the aeroplane?"

He sighs heavily and lets his head drop to my shoulder as though trying to hide his frustration. "Nel, it doesn't matter who I have or haven't been with in the past. All that matters is that I want you. I have for a long time, and I don't see that changing any time soon." Rolling his hips, he works the length of him along my sex and I gasp at the welcome friction. "I happen to think your body is hot as Hell." Another grind of his hips and I'm panting. I lift my legs and wrap them around his hips, using my heels to push his underwear off his arse and down his legs. "Your body does things to me, Nel." His voice seems to have dropped an octave and his bare cock rubs along my lower lips. "I want to leave my mark on every inch of you. I want to *worship* every inch of you. The more inches, the more there is to fucking worship."

My heart hammers and my tears make an appearance but not for the same reason. This man is perfect. "Jake, I need you inside me."

"But I didn't finish breakfast," he complains and quicker than I can process he's back between my legs. He's not teasing this time; he eats me out like a starved man. Deep laps of his tongue alternating with hard sucks on my clit have me coming in less than a minute. He's rushed and flustered when he sits up and fumbles with the condom before he's properly suited up. Just when I expect him to sink deep, he grabs my hips again and in an impressive show of strength, flips me to my stomach and hauls my butt up so I'm on my knees with my cheek against my pillow. Then, without further warning, he slams into me and curves himself over my back so his lips are by my ear. "You are perfect to me, Nel Forrest."

CHAPTER NINETEEN
"What the hell gave me away?"

JAKE

I really need to stop touching Nel. We decided to walk to Harry's so I didn't have to leave the car there overnight, and it was just too natural to slip my fingers in between hers as we walked. That quickly escalated to my arm around her waist, then my hand slid to rest on her butt, feeling the movement of each step and resisting the urge to drag her back to the hotel to go for round three. But we're spending the day with Harry and his family and Nel wants to keep things low key, which I'm happy to do for her.

I'd love to say she has nothing to worry about and that Harry will be fine, but he is a little weird about stuff sometimes. At least he is at first. Once he's had a moment to digest things, he often realises things are better than he thought. Like when Lisa told him he was going to be a dad for the third time and he had a mini meltdown because it was unplanned. Once his brain had a chance to evolve from its impulsive response, he realised that he loves being a father, he and Lisa are as strong as a couple can be and they're financially comfortable, he recognised it as being wonderful news.

We walk straight into the house which has been unlocked for us already. We kick off our shoes and when Nel steadies herself on the door frame while removing her boots, I can't help but steal a quick kiss as no one is in the hall to see us.

"Jake," she hisses, quickly checking for witnesses.

"Sorry, little elf. Got to follow the rules." I point up to the mistletoe above her head and make my way up the hall. "Merry

123

Christmas!" I call to find where everyone is and when it's repeated back to me in a cheerful chorus, I gesture for Nel to walk ahead of me into the kitchen where they seem to be. I stuff my hands in my pockets because it's all too easy to put one at the small of her back to guide her through the door, and I'm starting to think that today is going to be harder than anticipated.

"Uncle Jake!" Lucas runs over to me and bands his arms around my waist.

"Hey bud, you had a good morning?"

"Yeah! Wanna see what I got from Santa?"

"Not now, Lucas. It's breakfast time." Lisa comes from the garage carrying a huge platter of croissants and ushers him off before planting a quick kiss on my cheek. "Merry Christmas, Jake."

"Merry Christmas, Lis. Can I help with anything?"

"No, we're all good. Take a seat." She kisses Nel's cheek, too, and gives her a beautiful smile. At the table, Nel and I are greeted with well wishes and bright smiles. The twins are excitedly babbling, each sat with a grandparent while Oscar stands between Charles and Cami with his arms around their shoulders as they sit at the table.

"Hi Aunty Nels-Bels. Hi Uncle Jake," he waves animatedly at us.

"Hi Ozzy, Merry Christmas," Nel smiles sweetly at him.

"Hey, I hear you met Santa last night," I say to my youngest Godson.

He gives me an amused glare. "I know it was you, Uncle Jake."

"What was me?" I screw my face up in confusion.

"You were the Santa at the fair last night."

"What!?"

"Auntie Nel was the elf!" he accuses with the conviction of a courtroom drama.

As though practiced, Nel and I look at each other in perfect unison with mirroring facial expression of exaggerated horror.

"You were the elf?" I sneer.

"You were *Santa*?" she sobs.

"I know you're pretending," Oscar giggles.

"Hey, hey, hey!" Harry comes in from the garage with two pitchers of orange juice that he places on the table before giving me a back-slapping hug. "Merry Christmas, brother."

"Merry Christmas, mate. You good?" I ask him quietly as the smile on his face looks a little strained.

"Of course," he says brightly. He hugs Nel and kisses her cheek before herding his children to their seats.

As we sit down, Cami smiles at Nel and says, "You look absolutely stunning, Nel."

"Oh, thank you." She sits demurely, taking the compliment without her usual blush, just as she should. She looks fantastic in a crystal blue velvet dress that hugs her rocking curves, her hair is pinned up with a few loose strands falling around her face. As usual, her makeup is impeccable, and I'd like to think that the easy smile on her face might have something to do with the multiple orgasms she's had over the last twelve hours.

"Nel, you do look gorgeous," Lisa says as she takes her seat and places a plate of smoked salmon down. "Doesn't she, Jake?"

"Oh, yeah," I say, giving Nel an appreciative once over and that attractive pink is back in her cheeks as she bites her lip to try and hide her smile. I realise I may have been looking a little too carnal, so I clear my throat and add, "Everyone looks great."

"Yes, it's lovely when everyone makes an effort. Where was your effort?" Lis asks with mock curiosity, eyeing my jeans.

"I'm wearing a shirt," I say defensively, gesturing to my dark green button down that I usually only wear at work. "Plus, the itinerary didn't state a dress code, so who's really to blame here?"

"Idiot," she mumbles behind the rim of her coffee cup, but her smile is still visible. "Everyone, help yourselves," she says more loudly.

The table looks incredible, laden with smoked salmon, toasted bagels, cream cheese, coddled eggs, croissants, jams, butter, and pitchers of juice as well as two huge cafetieres of coffee and pots of tea.

"Lisa, this looks amazing," Nel says. "And I really love your dress."

Lis looks down at the red dress she wears with a scooped neckline and form fitting body that proudly displays her baby bump. "Oh, thank you! It's so hard to find nice maternity clothes and when I saw this, I actually thought of you. It looked like something you would wear."

Nel smiled again. "I would definitely wear something like that, It's very beautiful."

"Maybe you should give it to Nelly-Belly once you've had the baby, babe," Harry says as he passes the cream cheese.

I feel Nel flinch next to me and the table goes awkwardly silent. And not for the first time this weekend, I'm angry at my best friend. "Dude," I say in a tone that implies the '*what the fuck?*'

"What?" He looks at me wide eyed and genuinely baffled.

"Oh, Harry," Lisa sighs more to herself than to him, her disappointment obvious.

Nel's jaw is clenched and her eyes fixed on her empty plate, the genuine smile and easy confidence she's walked in with now lost. She doesn't want me to tell Harry he's a dick and she doesn't want to give the moment more time, so I do what I can to move on from it.

"So, Lucas, Oscar, what did Santa bring you?"

The boys are so excited to regale me with exact accounts of their morning so far that they're talking over each other and stumbling over their words. It takes no time at all for everyone

126

else to join in. Margot and Freddie are giggling ecstatically, basking in the attention of their parents and grandparents, and Lucas and Oscar start squabbling over who the electric car Santa brought was for. With everyone distracted, I rest my arm over the back of Nel's chair and lightly stroke the back of her neck with my thumb. Hoping the gesture tells her I'm here, that she's perfect, and that her brother is just an idiot. It's a lot to ask from one thumb stroke, but I'm hopeful we got there.

Lisa and Harry seem to be having a private conversation and I hear her say, "Think before you speak, darling." To which he only frowns and looks utterly confused.

Breakfast goes by quite quickly with never ending conversation and laughter. The boys drag Nel into their conversation which brightens her up again and she also has a serious discussion with Charles about her business and plans for the future. They're both using terminology that I don't totally understand and Nel seems to be giving answers to Charles' questions that impress him. Harry watches the exchange with his eyes dancing between them like he's at a tennis match.

"You're an impressive young lady, Penelope," Charles beams.

"Well, thank you," Nel blushes. "I don't think anyone has ever said that about me before."

"Maybe not to your face, but I have definitely been impressed by you," Lisa says to her, and Harry looks surprised by her words.

"Believe the compliments, little elf," I whisper to her when the hum of background chatter rises again. She smiles up at me, those chocolate-brown eyes wide under her dark lashes.

When plates are empty, coffee cups on their last dregs, Lisa stands to start clearing, Harry offers help but she tells him to relax and he gives me a look across the table. Our conversation the other night comes back to me, so without asking, I get up and start clearing plates. Nel does, too, but Lisa tells her to sit back down. We work in comfortable quiet, me clearing the table and

127

loading the dishwasher while Lisa checks the turkey in the oven and does a little more prep for lunch.

I'm putting the fancy Christmas crockery out in the garage where it's being kept until needed when Lisa comes out with a few dishes to store out here too.

"You and Nel seem to be getting on well," she says casually.

I'm not fooled by her tone. "Why wouldn't we?" I shrug.

"No reason. I just mean you seem particularly chummy. Have you two been spending time together at the hotel or something?"

I don't really know how to answer that, so I fold my arms and narrow my eyes at her.

She studies me for a moment before her eyes go wide and she gasps. "You slept with her, didn't you?"

My jaw drops.

"Don't lie to me, Jake Partridge." She points a manicured nail in my face.

"What the hell gave me away?" My hands drop to my side, defences down.

She just throws her head back and laughs. "I know you, Jake. Plus, it makes sense."

"It does?"

"Of course. She's obviously been crushing on you since she got her first training bra, and you've been in love with her for years."

Seriously. My jaw cannot get any lower. "Love?" I squeak and she just nods. "I think that might be a bit premature."

Lisa rolls her eyes but smiles and shakes her head. "Baby boy, you are clueless."

"We just started this; how could I have been in love with her already?"

"It is more than possible to be in love with someone without being with them. 'How's Nel?' is always one of the first questions you ask when you see Harry, and then you seem to know more about her then he does. You've clearly been cyber-stalking her, you weirdo." She winks at me to show she's joking.

My mouth is a little dry. "Still," I croak. "That doesn't mean love."

"Not necessarily," she agrees. "But I think it does in this instance."

I scrape my hand over my face, finding I can't disagree with her right now. "Don't say anything, okay?"

"Yeah," she sighs. "Probably best not to spring this on Harry right now."

I snort at that. "Well, he has only himself to blame."

"How's that?"

"He fucked up the hotel booking. They only had one room for both of us, so we've been sharing a room," I laugh.

She gasps in delight and claps her hands together. "One bed?"

I nod, snorting in amusement at her enthusiasm.

"Oh God, it's like a Christmas romance movie!"

"You're ridiculous."

"Seriously though," she says placing her hands on my shoulders. "I love this for you, both of you. Lord knows that girl needs some happy in her life right now and you deserve a fulfilling relationship."

I smile at her. "Love you, Lis."

"Alright, don't go getting squishy on me."

We hug and head back to the kitchen to continue the Christmas celebrations, and I feel as though a weight has been lifted.

CHAPTER TWENTY
"Oh, Jake's hot now?"

NEL

I hate to admit this, but this big family Christmas, complete with loud children and people talking over each other and forced socialising, is brilliant. After breakfast, the games started. We played a couple rounds of charades, and I discovered that the only thing worse than Charles and Gordan on a team together is Charles and Gordan on opposite teams. The gentle and always smiling brothers turn into the Kray twins with a little friendly competition. Their wives just roll their eyes and ignore their raucous banter while I was tearing up through my laughter.

"How is *this* Planet of the Apes?" Gordan yells, mimicking Charles' monkey impression.

"You just concentrate on your own team, little brother. My guys knew what I was doing."

"You keep telling yourself that, chimp boy."

"Just get on with your turn."

"Sure thing, Bubbles."

It goes on like that through charades, Wink Murder, and Pictionary. Musical Chairs got positively violent. Lisa has printed out actual cocktail menus and Rhiannon ropes me in to trying each of the seven offerings with her. We were halfway through the menu when we sat down to lunch, which consisted of every side dish imaginable to go with the biggest turkey I've ever seen. Once that was consumed and everyone practically rolled back into the lounge while Luke, Jake, and Harry did the washing up, we resumed our drinking challenge. When everyone joins us, Lucas proudly announces that it is time for presents and offers to play Santa, dishing them out. There are so many presents. Of course, most are for the kids and I feel relieved that I'd thought to buy little token gifts for Freddie and Margot as Jake had bought them things too.

I'm mortified when I'm given gifts from Charles and Cami, Gordan and Hen, and Rhiannon and Luke. I hardly know these people; I didn't think we would be doing presents. Of course, they all tell me not to worry, they didn't buy gifts to receive gifts but still, I feel like a class-A dick. The velvet makeup case from Rhiannon and Luke, the fancy bath stuff from Gordan and Hen, and the voucher for a popular chain restaurant—with enough on it for a two-course meal for two, plus drinks—from Charles and Cami are all so thoughtful and all things I will use. Man, I feel like shit.

"I'm so sorry I didn't get you all something," I say to the room and am met with protests of how it doesn't matter. "Cami, if you were serious and would like to do a family photo shoot, I'd love to do that for you all as your gift."

Everyone is enthusiastic with their response, and I beam, pleased to be able to do something.

Lisa's hand goes up like she's tentatively asking a question in class. "Can I ask that we wait until the baby is born so they can be in the shoot, and so I don't look like a hippopotamus in the photos?"

"Absolutely not," Rhiannon says, with a false sternness. "I happen to like you looking like a hippopotamus."

Lisa just rubs her eye with her middle finger in lieu of responding.

"Whenever you're all free, I'll make time. Maybe in the summer we could do something over in the common here. Easier for everyone to get to than London."

More presents are handed out and yet another one is placed in my lap. It's heavy but small and Lucas doesn't tell me who it's from before he's gathering another load of wrapped parcels to dole out. I check the label and smile.

Little Elf,

For when you need a little extra Christmas Spirit

Santa

X

I look at Jake but he is blowing raspberries on Freddie's tummy while he giggles uncontrollably and his twin bounces excitedly, waiting for her turn. Jake looks up briefly, catching my eye and winking before resuming his delightful torture. I don't even know when Jake would have had time to wrap a present, he didn't come with it this morning. I tug the wrapping paper to expose the plain brown box beneath, opening that, I pull out the polystyrene packaging and then have to pry that apart to reveal the snow globe I was expecting. Although, it isn't the one we'd seen yesterday. This one shows a figurine couple kissing, her leg kicked up, his arms around her waist. A Christmas tree sits next to them with brightly coloured decorations painted onto the green branches and the base the globe sits on is painted to look like antique brass with the words *Meet Me Under the Mistletoe* wrapped around its circumference.

I suspect Jake told Luke to hand this out when everyone else has a present, too, as no one takes note of the gift that brings me the most joy today. Good thing, as I'm sure it would raise a few eyebrows. All the gifts are distributed and there is a mass of colourful paper in the middle of the room, the children are all high on Christmas excitement, and it is chaotic to say the least. But I'm still okay with it; I'm enjoying the chatter, the buzz, and everyone's joy. I'm smiling when I lock gazes with Harry and he gives me the brightest smile back.

You good? he mouths at me.

I dip my head in a nod. *You?* I mouth back to him.

He gestures around the room, to the festive jubilance and shrugs as though that should answer the question.

It feels like the most meaningful conversation we've had and I resolve here and now to make more of an effort to see my brother and his family. I have apparently been missing out. When we all jump in to help get the lounge back to a usable state, I place all of my gifts in a gift bag and take it to the porch to leave next to my shoes for later. When I turn back to the hall, Jake is right in front of me.

"Jesus!" I gasp, clutching at my chest. "You scared me!"

He raises a dark brow and narrows his eyes. "That's the second time you've used another man's name when we're together, little elf."

"Who? Jesus?"

"Sanctimonious bastard," he scoffs, shaking his head.

"Oh, be nice," I chide. "It's his birthday."

He chuckles as he takes a small step forward so we are toe-to-toe, his hand coming out to stroke mine at my side. "Did I tell you how beautiful you look today?"

"I think you might have mentioned something when we left this morning," I smile at him.

"Hmm," he looks up thoughtfully. "Maybe I should tell you again, just to be on the safe side."

"Maybe," I shrug with as much nonchalance I can manage through the butterflies in my belly.

"Or, you know, I could show you," he grips my waist and pulls me flush against his body.

"Someone could see," I whisper but the argument is weak as my lips ghost his.

"You want to stop?" The amusement in his voice tells me that he knows I don't.

"Well, you are under the mistletoe, don't want bad luck or whatever."

"We certainly don't," he murmurs just as his lips meet mine. He's soft and gentle as he kisses me, sweet and tender. His tongue pushing lightly at the seam of my mouth, waiting for an invite, not claiming as he has done before. I let him in and moan softly as our tongues slide against one another.

"What the fuck!?"

We break apart but Jake's hands stay at my waist so we don't look guilty. Harry is stood in the hall, arms full of toys that he's likely meant to be taking upstairs. Instead, he's staring at us wide-eyed and open-mouthed.

"What. The. Fuck?" he says again, more anger in his voice, his eyes narrowing as he drops the toys into the corner so he can put his clenched fists on his hips.

"H," Jake starts cajoling.

"My sister, Jake? My *sister*?"

My stomach knots at the disgust in Harry's voice. His utter revulsion that his best friend would sink to settling for me.

"What the Hell is happening here?" Harry demands.

"What's wrong?" Lisa comes round the corner, looking at Harry with concern but when she sees Jake and I, she slows and lets out a knowing, "Ooooh."

Lisa knows?

"Babe, let's just take a minute to stay calm," Lisa places her hand gently on Harry's arm. He turns and glares at his wife, seeming to calculate something in his head before clenching his jaw tight.

"You knew about this?"

Her eyes flick to Jake and back. "Not exactly, but you know, it makes sense."

"How, Lisa? How does this make sense?" He gestures wide with his arms, confused by the whole situation.

She shrugs. "They're both young, single, and hot."

"Oh, Jake's hot now?" Harry sneers, his anger now being directed wherever is easiest.

Lisa isn't deterred by his attitude, rolling her eyes and sighing. "Yes, Harry. Jake is hot. Nel is hot. It makes sense they find each other hot."

My brother's face contorts as he seems appalled at the very idea and something in me snaps. I am so angry. Angry that the kinship we seemed to have just minutes ago is lost so quickly. Angry that I was enjoying this big family Christmas that I had been dreading for weeks only for it to be ruined. Angry that my brother doesn't think I'm good enough for his best friend.

"Honestly Harry, I know I'm not your favourite person in the world, but I didn't think I ranked so low that you'd be this upset about this." I'm impressed by the strength of my own voice.

"What?" He jerks back as my words hit him, the anger fading to give way for more confusion. It looks like he might say something else, but I don't give him the chance to continue.

"I get it, okay? I'm fat, you have reminded me at every opportunity." Shit, my eyes are starting to sting and I can feel the tears gathering, ready to spill. Harry's mouth gapes open, apparently shocked that I'm standing up for myself. Jake's hand slips into mine; a show of silent support. "And you've made it abundantly clear that you're ashamed of what I do. But honestly, I think everyone would be more offended by the fact you thought they'd judge me on it than they are by the fact I take photos of people in their underwear. Maybe I don't have my shit together all the time like you do, but *this*," I gesture between Jake and I, "has nothing to do with you. And you don't get to be mad at me for it."

Everyone is quiet for a long moment, digesting the situation and my outburst. Jake's hand tightens over mine and Lisa is giving me a proud smirk behind Harry's shoulder.

"What are you talking about?" Harry screws his face up. "You think I'm ashamed of you?" The hurt in his voice takes me aback slightly, my shoulders dropping an inch. "I'm not ashamed of you, Nellie."

"Then what's your problem?" I blink and the threatening tears overflow, my voice cracking slightly. I'm unsure if my emotions are anger or relief that my brother doesn't think I'm a complete fuck-up.

"Him!" Harry shouts, gesturing to Jake.

"What?!" Jake, Lisa, and I all say at the same time.

"Dude, I love you but you kind of get around a bit."

"Oh what, and you never had casual sex before you got married?" Jake says with more snap than I've heard him talk to Harry with before.

"You're going to marry my sister now?" Harry snarks back.

"Maybe!" Jake shouts.

"Whoa, let's all just calm down," I interrupt before my heart gives out completely.

"You know every time things start to look a little serious with a girl, he bails?" Harry says to me.

My cheeks flush and I look to the floor because I don't know what to say to that.

Lisa claps her hands together once and gets everyone's attention. "Okay, we're all going to take a breath. Nel, come with me. Harry, talk to your friend and apologise for being a dick. Then come find Nel to do the same."

Lisa practically shoves Harry at us and holds her hand out to me, which I take, letting her lead me to the kitchen.

CHAPTER TWENTY-ONE
"Don't say flesh when you're talking about my sister."

JAKE

"**W**hat the actual fuck, Harry?" Okay, I'm pissed. I knew Harry would be a little surprised. I knew he would probably react poorly to begin with. I knew his anger would be with me, not Nel no matter what she thought. But outright saying I'm not good enough is a major kick in the balls. I mean, this guy is meant to be my best friend, my ride or die, the Goose to my Maverick. Not the guy shitting on me for being a little fast and loose with Little Jake over the years. Seriously, the guy was basically Casanova at university before he met Lisa. Where does he get off judging me?

"Not here," he says, grabbing our coats from the hooks and throwing mine at me. "Outside."

We head out the door and I look back to see if I can catch Nel's eye to see if she's okay, but she and Lisa have long gone. The air is bitter and the sun has set, so we walk up the street by the light of Pear Street's Christmas lights.

"H," I sigh, trying to lose some of my anger. "Is that really what you think of me?"

He groans and shoves his hands in his pockets. "I'm sorry, dude. That all came out wrong."

"Well, how was it supposed come out, Harry?" I start walking at a slow pace. He huffs, clearly uncomfortable and unsure of how to respond, so I give him a break and start this conversation off. "I know you're protective of Nel, it's natural, she's your little sister. But mate, you know you can't be mad with this, right? We've not done anything wrong."

He stops to look at me, we've barely made it past the front of his massive house, walking at such a slow pace. His head hangs, takes a deep breath and lets it out before looking back up to meet my eye. "Nel barely sees me right now. She's always too busy or too tired to come out to us, and when we lost Mum and Dad, it got worse. I had to beg to get her here and I think she's enjoyed it. I want her to come by more often, have more of a relationship with the boys, and I think that's more likely now she's spent Christmas with us. But it won't happen if you fuck this up."

What he's saying makes sense, but I still can't help the punch to my gut. "And you think I'm going to fuck this up." It's not a question, he basically just told me as much. Me and Nel.

He looks at me helplessly. "Come on man, you've broken up with every girl who ever got slightly attached."

"Isn't every relationship unsuccessful until you find the one that succeeds?"

"So Nel's the one, is she?" he asks sceptically.

"I don't know dude," I shrug. "Before this weekend, I hadn't seen her in the flesh for years."

He screws his face up. "Don't say flesh when you're talking about my sister."

I snort and continue walking along the pavement. "But you should know, I've been following her on social media. I lied before when I said I'd seen one or two posts; I've seen them all. I kind of became enraptured by her. I meant it when I said you should check out her posts, H. I think she's a wildly different person to the sister you think you know."

He still looks unsure, stopping his steps and looking out to the road in contemplation.

"I know I haven't given any other girl a shot in recent years but honestly, H, I've kind of been falling for Nel. Just from a distance."

"Falling for her?" His head snaps back to look at me and his eyes go wide.

"Yeah, your wife tells me I'm in love."

That makes him laugh. "Yeah, she's good like that, tells you how you're feeling and the next thing you know, you're feeling it."

"Dude, she might be a witch," I say, putting a little fear into my voice.

"Oh, she definitely is," he says with a seriousness.

"I'm sorry you were blindsided, mate. That wasn't the intention. But you know me, you know I'm not going to screw over Nel." We stare at each other for a few seconds while he seems to digest that.

"Do you love her?" he asks gently.

I blow out a breath and look to the pavement beneath my feet. Shit, am I blushing?

Harry laughs before I can answer. "Oh, bloody hell."

"What?"

"You're totally falling in love with my sister." He scrubs his palm down his face.

I put my hands on my hips and hang my head, trying to word this properly. I'm not going to tell Harry I'm in love with his sister, not until I've told Nel, at least. "This is all very new, Harry. I can't tell you what's going to happen in the next few weeks, months, years. But I can tell you that Nel means a lot to me, that I'm serious about her, and that I will not fuck this up. Not intentionally, anyway."

He nods, seeming to accept what I'm telling him. "Good, because I'd hate to have to kick your arse."

I snort. "Sure, like you could."

"I could totally take you."

"I would destroy you."

"You would fold so quickly."

"You would be crying like a little girl."

We smile.

"Are we good?" I ask.

"Have you forgiven me for being a dick?"

"Been doing that for years, mate."

"Arsehole."

"Prick."

We smile again.

"We're good. I'm sorry I reacted poorly."

"I'm sorry I'm going to be banging your sister for the foreseeable."

"Maybe we're not so good," he grumbles.

I chuckle. "I love you, H."

"I love you too, dickhead."

"You want to go back in? Ready for apology number two?" I smirk at him and he rolls his eyes, but he heads back toward the house with a slap on my back.

"All joking aside, mate, if you hurt Nel, I *will* break your pretty face."

CHAPTER TWENTY-TWO
"I think we both need to stop apologising,"

NEL

L isa leads me away from Harry and Jake toward the kitchen. I look back to catch Jake's eye, but Harry is between us, shoving a coat into Jake's chest. We go to the garage to Lisa's little prep station and she starts pulling platters out of a fridge and arranging snacks on them. *Holy Hell, more food?* We're silent for a little while, letting my mind wonder to what just happened.

Harry seemed hurt at the thought of me believing him to be ashamed of me, his green eyes looking so pained. The concept of Jake not being good enough for me is not sinking in. That is the complete opposite of fact. Jake is the whole package complete with ribbon, I'm missing items and lost in the post. I wonder what they're saying to each other right now.

"He loves you, you know?" Lisa says, her back to me as she busies herself with cheese and crackers.

"Jake?" I squeak.

She chuckles. "Sure. But I was talking about Harry."

I sag a little in relief, I'm pretty sure. Jake and I haven't even been on a date yet, it would weird to be talking about love. "I know Harry loves me," I say.

"Do you?" She still isn't looking at me, so I frown at her back. What an odd question. "You know that he loves you as a sibling should, but do you know that he cares about you more than he lets on?"

"I care about him too," I mumble.

She finally turns around and faces me with a warm smile. "I know, Nel. Harry's been worried about you after your parents." I swallow down the familiar ball of emotion at the mention of Mum and Dad. "He doesn't always know how to be there for people and he usually speaks without thinking but he wants to be there for you, Nel."

I blink at her, still unsure of what to say, so I just wait for her to continue.

"He might have told you that I wanted to make your mum's pie for you, and it was absolutely true, but he was the one who suggested it. He was the one who went through all her old handwritten recipes to find the right one. He was also the one to tell Rhiannon and Luke to stay here to give you the excuse to stay at the hotel, he knew you'd be more comfortable there."

My eyes well and my lips tremble. I honestly had no idea Harry cared that much. I didn't realise he was anything but annoyed at me.

"And look at how well that turned out for you," Lisa smirks and I blush. "Harry doesn't have a problem with you and Jake."

"Definitely sounded like he does," I laugh without humour.

She shrugs, not worried at all. "He just doesn't like to be surprised and you surprised him. I mean, you could have kept your hands to yourself while you were here," her words are scolding but there's no anger, she just laughs.

"It was Jake!" I defend.

"Because he is seriously into you." I blush again. "Don't let your inner demons drown out the reality, Nel."

"What makes you say that?"

She shrugs again. "I've known you a while, even if I don't see you that often." She hadn't meant that as a dig but it still thumped at my chest.

"I'm sorry I don't come by," I say to the ground.

She waves a hand and makes a dismissive sound. "I get it, it's loud and chaotic in this house most of the time."

"Still, I've been a kind of shitty sister."

"Yeah, well, Harry can be a shitty brother sometimes." When I raise my brows at her she gives another little chuckle. "I see it. But he doesn't mean it."

The door between the garage and the kitchen opens and my brother stands there, wearing his black coat, holding my beige one. His cheeks are ruddy from the cold, the tips of his ears pink, and his hair a little wild where he's obviously been running his hand through it.

"Can we talk?" he says to me. I nod and take my coat from him; over my shoulder he looks at his wife. "You okay, babe?"

"I'm absolutely fine. Go talk to you sister and come back to snuggle with me on the sofa."

I catch his sweet smile for her before I pass him and put my coat on. I expect Harry to lead me out the front as he did with Jake, but he steers me to the patio doors at the back of the house where my boots are already waiting for me. He says nothing as he slides the door shut behind us, nor when he trots down the steps of the patio to the grass. I follow him, feeling nervous, not unusual since I often get a little thrum of nerves when I talk to my brother, waiting for the berating I'm sure to get.

We walk all the way to the end of the garden, where it's nearly pitch black and the grass gives way to another small patio area. Harry flops down on the large, wood framed bench swing and I follow suit. The wood creaks as we gently sway back and forth, and Harry looks dead ahead to the back of the house aglow from the lights inside. The nervous little sister inside me wants to say something to kill this buzzing silence. But I wait.

And wait.

"When Oscar was a baby, he had a fever." I jerk back, completely thrown off by his choice of subject, but I let him continue. "He was screaming in the middle of the night; his

143

temperature was seriously high and he was arching his back. We were really worried so I took him to A&E while Lis stayed home with Lucas. We were put in a bay where they took some blood for tests and I was waiting on my own and trying to stay calm for Oscar but I was freaking out." His voice hitches, the memory clearly still upsetting. "I called Mum, thinking she probably wouldn't be up, but she answered on the second ring. She had been up binge-watching the first season of Game of Thrones and hadn't realised the time."

I laugh at that. "What, just seven years behind everyone else?"

Harry chuckles. "Yeah, she loved what everyone else loved, just after they'd stopped loving it." We each smile at our own memories for a few moments before he continues. "I called her to chat, to get my mind off the situation, but I was so tired and worried that I just broke down. She told me everything would be alright and all the usual things. Then she told me about when you were two and cracked your head open at the pool. Do you remember that?"

I thought about it for a second. "I remember people telling me about it, but I don't think I remember it."

"We were at the lido and I was chasing you around, you slipped and hit your head on the side of the pool. Dad wasn't there, it was just Mum and she freaked out, it looked like so much blood. Retrospectively, it was probably because there was water on the ground that made it look worse than it was but still, Mum bundled us up and went to the hospital. You were in a state, screaming and crying, probably feeding off Mum's panic. You only stopped crying when I got into the hospital bed with you and held you."

I don't remember being told about that; I don't remember ever being that close with Harry.

"Mum reminded me of this," Harry continues and wipes at his cheeks. He's crying and it tears at my heart. Shuffling closer to him, I instinctively wrap my arm around his back. "Then she told me that while we were lying together, she sang The Ugly Bug Ball."

"The what now?" I ask, scrunching my face up.

Harry lets out a little laugh. "It's from some old movie she loved and apparently at the time, it was the only thing she could think of, so she sang it to us." He swallows audibly and takes a moment before continuing, his voice cracking over the words. "So, while I was sat with Oscar in a hospital bay at two o'clock in the morning, I put the phone on speaker and she sang the stupid ugly bug song. Oscar fell asleep and I felt calm in the midst of the madness." He sniffs and wipes his face again. "Sometimes I get a random memory of that night and I can even hear Mum singing to the point that I can hum along, and it always makes me smile." He finally turns to look at me and the soft light from the house catches on the wetness of his cheek. "Nel, I'm really scared that one day I won't be able to hear her singing anymore." He breaks, his head hanging and his shoulders shaking as he cries. He cries more than I ever saw him cry and my heart breaks for him.

"Oh, Harry," I wrap my arms around his neck and he rests his head on my shoulder, hugging me back. "I'm so sorry."

"Why are you sorry?" His words come out muffled against my coat.

"I'm sorry I didn't realise you were struggling."

We pull apart and he wipes the tears on my cheeks, both of us laughing. "Of course, I'm struggling, Nel. We lost both our parents in twelve months. I think anyone would struggle with that."

I take a deep breath and expel it, hoping to steady my voice. "Why didn't you tell me?"

He turns to look back at the house, composing himself and seeming to think about how to answer that. "You were struggling, too, and I didn't want to add to that. I wanted to be strong for you. For my family."

I think back to the time after losing Mum. The funeral where I hid in the wardrobe, the probate meeting where I said nothing then ran home to cry by myself, leaving Harry to be by himself. "I'm really sorry I made you feel like that was something you had to do, Harry."

He shrugs like it's no big deal. But it is a big deal. I resent Harry for treating me like a child but when he needed me to step up and be an adult, I let him down. "I miss you, Nel. I miss seeing you, I miss talking to you. I'm not entirely sure what went wrong but I have a feeling it's my fault."

I shake my head. "It's not your fault, Harry. It's just…"

"You think I'm ashamed of you and it makes me hard to be around," he finishes for me, defeatedly.

I go to disagree but stop myself. "I feel like I'm being judged a lot when I'm around you. You don't like my job, you think I'm immature for living with housemates, you think I'm a loner, you use me as the butt of your jokes that usually revolve around me being fat. It's just a lot to take and I need a lot of mental preparation to be here. Mum and Dad used to be my buffers and now I feel like I'm facing it all on my own."

He sighs, deeply. "Shit. That's hard to hear."

I nod.

"I'm sorry Nelly-Belly."

"Harry. Nelly-Belly has got to go."

"What's wrong with Nelly-Belly?" He sits up straight, genuinely clueless.

"Remember when you started calling me that? When I wore a bikini for a first time?" He looks at me blankly. "France? You were trying to impress those boys playing football because you wanted them to invite you to play."

He looks off into the distance, searching for the memory. "Oh shit. I'd completely forgotten that. I really am a shitty brother, aren't I?"

I chuckle thinking of Lisa's words before Harry came to collect me. "You're not a shitty brother. And I'm not a shitty sister. We just need to find our vibe again."

"I don't judge you, Nel. I worry about you, and I guess it comes out wrong sometimes."

"What are you worried about?" I ask, hoping to maybe alleviate some of his concerns.

He sighs again. "You were so dependent on Mum and Dad; I know you don't have many other people—"

"What makes you think that?"

"Uh…I guess, just that I've never met any of your friends and you never really talk about them."

"I have friends, Harry. My roommates are my friends, I have people from uni that I still see, and I have clients who became good friends. I see them, talk to them, go out for dinners, coffee. I was *close* to Mum and Dad, Harry, I wasn't dependent on them."

"How come I've never met them?"

I squeeze my hands between my legs to try and warm them up and suck in air through my teeth. "As we've already established the names, the teasing, the judgement makes me uncomfortable and I don't want to be like that around my friends. I don't feel like I'm that person anymore. Only when I'm here."

"I'm sorry, Nel. And I'm sorry about the jokes. I honestly thought you were laughing with me."

"I know. I think we both need to stop apologising," I chuckle.

"One more?"

I nod.

"I'm sorry I reacted poorly to you and Jake; it was…a shock."

"To you and me both," I laugh.

"It might take some getting used to but if you're happy, I'm happy."

"I am."

147

"I told him if he ever hurt you, I'd break his face."

That makes me laugh, loudly. "Oh my God, that is so cringey."

"Maybe, but it's true."

CHAPTER TWENTY-THREE
"I'm a man-friend now?"

JAKE

O scar and Lucas are calling me from the lounge but I'm skulking in the kitchen like a busy body. I've been pretending to wash the same glass for about ten minutes. I know Harry took Nel out to the back garden to talk and I'm trying to see them through the kitchen window but they've gone right to the bottom of the garden. I'm more nervous for him to be speaking to her than I was for him to speak to me.

"You know, a watched pot never boils," Lisa says, emerging from the garage with yet more snacks.

"God, woman. You trying to kill us all with food?"

"No one goes hungry in my house, Partridge."

I take the giant plate from her and place it on the dining table. She disappears again, returning a moment later with another platter filled with cheese and crackers.

"Don't look at me like that, it's Christmas! Eat, drink, and be merry and all that. Rhiannon has done the drinking, she's a little too merry and needs to eat to soak it all up."

On cue, Rhiannon starts singing *Simply Having a Wonderful Christmas Time* loudly and out of tune from the lounge. Lisa gives me an *I told you so* look and I can only chuckle.

"You nervous?" she asks gently, jerking her head to the patio doors.

"No," I lie with false confidence.

"You and Harry okay?"

"Yeah," I sigh. "We're fine. I just need *them* to be fine too."

"They'll be fine. Those two just need their heads knocked together."

"And I'm sure you'd be happy to do that for them, violent wench."

"Speaking of violent," she turns to face me and crosses her arms over her chest. "You couldn't keep your hands to yourself for one day so this had to all go down on Christmas day?"

My lip quirks. "Sorry. I got carried away."

"You going to admit you love her yet?" She smirks back at me.

"Not to you." I bop her nose.

"Spoil sport. But you should know, I'm really happy for you, Jake."

"Thanks, *babe*." I sling my arm around her shoulders as she tsks me. "You've done an incredible job of this weekend, Lis. You should be proud of yourself."

"Thank you. I just hope those two had fun," she says, motioning to the dark garden.

"I think they have. Harry was the winner of hide and seek and he won't shut up about it and Nel's been giggling with Rhiannon over fruity cocktails all afternoon. That's a great Christmas all around."

"I love you, Jake. You're not just Harry's best man-friend you know?"

"I'm a man-friend now?"

"Yeah, you're certainly not my boyfriend but you're more than just a friend to Harry. You're a man-friend." She shrugs and I smile down at her.

"Well, you're my best friend too. I won't be calling you a woman-friend though, makes me sound like an elderly widower looking for new love."

"You are old," she muses.

"I'm a whole three months older than you!"

"Mmm, old."

"Wench."

"Codger."

We both smile, looking out to the infinite blackness beyond the patio doors. After a beat, I can see Lisa wince and stretch from side to side to try and alleviate some kind of pain.

"Come on, you and *the bump* need a rest. Go sit down and just tell people to come in and help themselves. And people have been here for days now, if they want a drink, they know where everything is."

She squeezes my arm and gives me a thankful smile before heading into the lounge with everyone else. I hear her pass on the message that the food is a help-yourself situation, and I'm not surprised when no one rushes to the kitchen. The turkey and all the trimmings are still keeping everyone full and satisfied.

The patio door slides open and Nel and Harry walk through. Despite the smiles on their faces, I look at Nel for any sign of distress. "Are you okay?" I ask her.

I see Harry roll his eyes in my peripheral. "We were having a conversation, not a boxing match."

Nel chuckles at her brother before turning to me. "I'm fine. Just a little cold."

It would be really easy to offer to warm her up but I think that might be a little too much, too soon for Harry. He seems to understand my thought process though because he screws his face up in disgust and wanders into the lounge muttering something about not being drunk enough for this. Nel and I chuckle, left alone in the kitchen.

"Are *you* okay?" she asks me.

"Peachy," I reply with a smug smile that has her gaze dropping to my mouth and her lip clenched between her teeth.

"What Harry said…" she starts as though to defend him but trails off, unsure what to say, but I take her face in my hands.

151

"Harry and I are good, don't you worry, little elf." She smiles, her cheeks moving beneath my palms.

"Apparently he's going to mess you up if you make me cry." Her amused smirk tells me her money would be on me in that altercation.

I smile back at her and lean down so our lips are a breath apart. "If I hurt you, I'll let him." I kiss her gently and she leans into me, returning my kiss with delicate flicks of her tongue against my lips. I grant her access as my hands roam to find the soft curvature of her arse and squeeze at her cheeks with some force.

Smiling against me, she interrupts our little tongue tango to say, "This is how we got into trouble in the first place, Mr. Partridge."

"Yeah, we should probably get back in there before someone comes and catches us being naughty again."

"Bad form to be naughty at Christmas."

I take a step back before we start sucking face again but take her hand in mine and bring her knuckles to my lips. "Don't worry, little elf. Santa's taking the day off."

She chuckles as I plant a reverent kiss on the back of her hand.

We sit separately when we get back into the lounge, but my eyes keep being drawn to Nel. She seems so relaxed, so open. We're playing more games but Oscar has lost interest and sits cross legged between Nel's legs where she's sat on the floor, her back against the couch where Harry sits. Oscar is reading a book while Nel tickles at his back absentmindedly while laughing at Rhiannon trying to hum a tune for us all to guess and getting more and more frustrated when we can't interpret her drunken warbling.

The twins fall asleep in the middle of the room snuggling into each other and looking all kinds of cute in their little matching Christmas outfits. Luke picks up Margot to take her to bed and I automatically do the same to Freddie, cradling the little one to my shoulder.

"You two coming up to bed?" I look at my Godsons, Oscar struggling to keep his eyes open and Lucas is still practically vibrating with energy. He looks to his mother in question and she doesn't give him the answer he wants.

"I think it's time for bed, bub."

"Okay," he says but with an attitude that says he is far from okay with it.

"Come on, buddy." I hold my hand out to him and he does the same for Oscar so we follow Luke up the stairs in a chain. I let the boys do their thing in the bathroom while I follow Luke to one of the spare rooms and lay Freddie down next to Margot on the double bed to strip her and put her into pyjamas.

"You need a hand?" Despite the fact that the kids fell asleep amongst the revelry downstairs, not even disturbed by their mother's awful attempts at musicality, I find myself whispering here in the quiet of this room.

"Nah, you're fine," Luke matches my whisper. "Thanks for bringing him up, I don't think Rhiannon was in the best state," he chuckles.

"She's certainly having a good time."

"She is, she deserves it too." The smile on his face portrays the utter adoration he has for his wife and my mind goes straight to Nel again, wondering if my face lights up like that when I think of her.

"I'll leave you to it then," I say, shaking the mushy thoughts from my head.

The boys are in their room—well, it's Oscar's room as Lucas' room is being used for Gordan and Hen—and in their pyjamas when I get there.

"Alright, what story are we reading?" I ask, going to the bookshelf.

"I'm okay without a story, Uncle Jake," Lucas yawns.

153

"Well, it's not just about you," I say softly, turning to look at Lucas but he just jerks his head to Oscar's bed, where Oscar is out cold. "Oh."

"I don't like Oscar's books, they're too young for me."

"Okay, well Hen and Gordan are still downstairs, want me to go into your room and get one of your books?"

"Nah, I'm okay."

I go and sit on the side of his bed. "You had a good Christmas, bud?"

"Yeah," he says with a sleepy smile, his energy from downstairs depleting now he's snuggled under his duvet. "It was so cool having everyone here." His smile drops, a deep v forming between his brows.

"What's up?"

"I did miss Nanny and Poppa though."

His lips pull down at the corners and I reach out to stroke his hair. "I know, mate."

"Usually we spend Christmas with Nanny and Poppa and Aunty Nelly-Belly *or* Grandma and Grandad and Aunty Rhi. I liked that everyone was here together, and it was really cool that you were here too."

I place my hand to my chest. "I'm cool?"

"Yeah," he giggles.

"Well, I thought it was really cool being here with you too."

"Aunty Nelly should come here more, she's fun." His eyes close as he speaks.

"I think she's fun too, maybe you'll see more of her now."

"Cool," he sighs and I know he's a goner.

"Night, bud," I whisper, getting up from his bed and giving his hair another stroke. I check on Oscar and pull his duvet down a couple inches so it's not covering his nose before I switch out the light and shut their door.

Back downstairs, Nel has moved to the two-seater sofa and Rhiannon is lying on the floor with her arms upstretched to the ceiling, talking quite loudly, everyone chuckling at her. I flop onto the sofa next to Nel and Luke comes in and frowns down at his wife.

"What *are* you doing?"

"I'm telling Lis and Harry what mural they should paint on their ceiling," she says like it's the most normal thing in the world.

"Of course you are." He sits down on one of the dining chairs brought in for additional seating.

My hand naturally migrates to Nel's thigh, resting on her leg before I've even realised what I've done. She doesn't flinch or move away so I let it rest there while we continue watching the other interactions in the room.

"I think, my darling, you might be a little bit sozzled," Gordan tells his daughter.

Nel giggles, her head falling to my shoulder.

"Are you a little sozzled too, little elf?" I murmur against her hair, quietly enough for only us to hear. She nods and giggles again.

"I'll have you know," Rhiannon says, sitting up and swaying slightly. "I am pleasantly pickled. Nel and I were testing the cocktails. Someone had to do it, didn't they Nel?" She turns to us and does a comical double take at our position. "Whoa," she points at us.

"What's up, Rhi?" I chuckle.

"I knew it!" she shrieks.

"What?" Hen asks, looking between us all confused.

"Nel and Jake are finally together?" She looks back at us in question.

"Haven't they always been?" Hen asks, even more confused.

"No, Mum."

"Oh, well I thought they were," she says talking about us like we're not in the room. "They were both at the hotel together and they share all those private looks and secret conversations."

"We do not have private looks and secret conversations!" Nel laughs.

"Yes, you do," Rhiannon, Hen, Cami, and Lisa all say in almost perfect unison.

I look at the men in the room, all looking decidedly blank. I turn to Nel as she turns to me and we lock eyes, her smile growing and mine following suit.

"See!" Rhiannon points at us accusingly.

We both laugh and I squeeze her thigh. Harry is watching us closely his lips quirking up slightly as his sister laughs and kicks gently at Rhiannon's leg. My heart is full.

CHAPTER TWENTY-FOUR
"I will actually suffocate you."

NEL

"Exactly how drunk are you?" Jake asks me as we come through our hotel room door.

"Could probably complete a crossword, shouldn't drive a car," I answer.

"Good enough for me." He spins me so my back is to the door and pushes himself against my body, his mouth sealing over mine with barely restrained need. Jake pushes my coat from my shoulders and pulls at my dress so the hem goes from a very respectful knee length to a very revealing, barely covering my pussy length. While his lips trail along my cheek and jaw, his fingers knead at the back of my thighs. I yank his coat off him and tug at his shirt until it untucks from his jeans, my nails find the bare skin of his abs and scrape over the hard ridges, revelling in the way his muscles tremble at my touch.

"You look so fucking good in this dress," he growls against my neck as his hands skim over my hips and waist up to my breasts where he pulls down the wrap around front so my sapphire satin bra is on full display. "Fuck," he sighs. "Your tits."

"You can, if you want." I smirk at him. There's a tingling under my skin as I wait in anticipation for him to keep touching me, kissing me.

He raises a single dark eyebrow at me. "Duly noted."

Kissing the swell of my breasts, he pulls my dress up to my waist and sinks to his knees. He unzips and pulls off each of my boots, then the socks I wore underneath before he painfully slowly traces the tips of his fingers from my ankle to my knees.

I giggle and let out a very unsexy snort when he tickles behind my knee. He chuckles when I slap my hand over my mouth to try and catch the sound.

"That is the cutest noise."

"Shut up."

Placing featherlight kisses on the inside of my thighs, he hooks one knee from behind and places it over his shoulder, opening me up for him. He buries his nose in the apex of my thighs where my underwear covers me and breathes me in.

"Mmmm, you're so wet for me," he rumbles.

"Hard not to be when you're on your knees for me."

He hooks his finger in my satin panties and pulls them to one side so I'm completely exposed to him. Placing light kisses to my outer lips, he teases me by avoiding all the areas I want him to touch. I thread my fingers through his thick hair and try grinding myself into his mouth, but he holds steady.

"So impatient, little elf."

"You're killing me, Jake. Please."

"Hm, please what?"

"Please…just, please," I whine.

"Tell me what you want, Nel. You know how this works."

"Eurgh," I grunt in frustration. It only makes him look up at me with those whiskey eyes and Elvis smile, making my need pulse straight to my clit. "Lick me," I moan. "Make me come, Jake. Please."

Just when I think he's going to give me what I want, he removes my leg from his shoulder, stands, and pulls my dress completely off so I'm left in my cute, matching bra and panties. Taking my hand, he leads me to the bed and then starts unbuttoning his shirt. I watch with avid fascination as each inch of skin is revealed. He has a light dusting of dark hair on his chest and not an ounce of fat on him. Everything is lean muscle and lightly tanned skin. When his shirt is off, he removes his black leather belt, making a satisfying wisp as it slides through the loops. He unbuttons his jeans but doesn't unzip them and kicks off his shoes before removing his socks. He climbs onto the bed, resting his head in the centre of the pillows.

"Come sit on my face, little elf."

I blanche. "Absolutely not."

"Why not?"

"I will actually suffocate you."

"And I will die a happy man," he says with all seriousness.

"Jake," I protest.

"Nel, you want to come, so sit on my face and I'll make sure you do."

He really doesn't get it. "Jake, I don't think I have the muscle strength to hover for long."

Propped on his elbows, he gives me what I can only assume is the stern look he uses on students, and it does all kinds of funny things to me. "Did I say hover, Nel? Sit on my goddam face."

His voice brooks no argument, so I reluctantly start to climb up onto the bed but he stops me, demanding I remove my underwear first. I shimmy out of my knickers but leave my bra on for now, wouldn't want him to look up and see my wayward tits flinging around while I ride his face. Despite my reservations, a jolt of excitement zips through me as I climb over him until my knees are on the pillows either side of his head. He wraps an arm around each of my thighs and pulls me down until my centre meets his waiting mouth.

The gasp that I suck in brings cool air to my lungs, starkly contrasting with the prickly heat burning at my skin. Jake's beard is both rough and soft against my most sensitive flesh, scraping back and forth over my pussy as he works his mouth over me. His tongue swirls around my entrance like he's trying to lick every last drop of honey from the jar, making my eyes roll to the back of my head from the sensation. My hips are moving of their own volition, rocking minutely against his skilled mouth. He lets out a soft groan and I panic for a second thinking I really am

159

smothering him, but when I try to lift my weight from him, he just pulls me down further.

"Jake…God…I'm so close…" I pant as his tongue spears into me.

I'm burning up, my skin glowing from the thin sheen of sweat coating it, my heart pumping and my lower belly clenching. I'm riding to the cliff edge, hanging on to the plush velvet headboard for dear life. If I'd wanted to keep any of my weight off of Jake, I couldn't. My legs are slowing turning to jelly, my spine curling in as Jake grips the fleshiest parts of my arse with bruising force and sucks on my clit, pushing me over the cliff and into the glittering abyss of orgasm.

I lift just enough for Jake to shuffle out from under me, then I'm slumped with my forehead leaning on my arms resting on the top of the headboard. He's at my back as soon as he can be, the heat of his bare chest scorching against my sweat cooled skin. I'm caged in by his arms and unable to move due to his proximity and the fact that all my bones are now made of porridge. A shiver runs down my spine as his lips coast over my shoulders and his hands run up my arms to the clasp of my bra. I think I make a tiny whimper of a protest, but my reservations about being totally naked in front of him seem to have been obliterated by the best orgasm of my life.

When he slides my bra down my arms, my breasts fall heavy from my chest, but he soon takes their weight, holding them in his palms and massaging roughly. I turn to face him and he captures my lips with his, the taste of my cum on his tongue, his lips, his mouth is drugging. I reach behind me and push at his jeans and boxers to free the straining rod he's grinding into me; I stroke him with firm but slow movements while we kiss like we've all the time in the world.

"I want my mouth on you now," I whisper against his lips.

"Next time," he pecks my lips. "Right now, I need inside your tight little cunt."

I reach over to the box of condoms still on the bedside table and pass him one. He's quick to roll it on and gently probes at my entrance before he seems to think better of it and shuffles away.

"On your back, little elf."

I sort of collapse on to the mattress—because, you know, porridge bones—and settle my head on the pillows before he leans over me and kisses me again. His lips are tender on mine, his tongue stroking reverently into my mouth and his kiss gives me all the words we shouldn't be ready to say yet. But I know what he's telling me and I do everything I can to say it back. He shimmies the rest of the way out of his jeans so we're both completely bare to each other, except the thin layer of latex between us. Suddenly, that feels like too much, like I need the connection of flesh on flesh.

Just before he can push himself in, I stop him with a hand to his hip. "Jake…"

"What's wrong?" His brow pinches in concern.

I smile. "Nothing. But um…" Okay, when it comes to saying it out loud, my cheeks are flushing.

"Tell me, Nel." He nuzzles my neck and I can tell that he's desperate to be inside me but holding himself back for me.

"I'm on the pill, if you wanted to go… bare?"

He freezes, every muscle going rigid, and I worry that we may not be in the same place. I'm thinking of how to back pedal when he lifts his head to look at me and the pure heat in his eyes placates my pesky anxiety.

He opens his mouth as if to say something but closes it again and swallows. "I've never done that."

I shake my head. "Neither have I. But I think it's what I want. I mean, I *know* it's what I want, with you."

He darts his tongue out to wet his lips and gives a small nod, before sitting back on his heels and slowly pulling the condom off, keeping his eyes locked on mine the whole time as if waiting for me to change my mind. I don't. Leaning back over me, resting all his weight on one forearm while the other hand guides his bare crown to my core.

"You're perfect, little elf," he whispers, before pushing all the way in, in one hard and controlled thrust.

We both moan as he fills me, the raw connection feels so much better than anything I've had before. "Jake, this feels—

"—amazing," he finishes for me. He's slow, controlled, and intense as he fucks me. It doesn't feel like fucking at all.

"Jake, I—"

"I do too, baby." He captures my lips and kisses me in the same way he makes love to me. His bare cock slides over the hyper-sensitive spot inside me and I fall once again with Jake's name on my lips. He follows after me, breathing heavy into the crook of my neck and nipping at my earlobe.

An hour later, we're showered, in our pyjamas, and cuddled as close as two people can be. Jake's fingers trail patterns over my naked shoulders.

"Today didn't go quite how I was expecting."

"I'm sorry, that's my fault." He kisses the top of my head. "Are you mad?"

"No," I chuckle. "You still want to take me out in the New Year?"

"Yep," he answers immediately.

I bite my lip, my smile still fighting through. "So, are you, like, my boyfriend now?"

"Yep." Again, his answer comes with no hesitation and my heart bursts.

I roll over him and kiss him with everything I have. "Merry Christmas, Santa."

His smile is devastating as he brushes my hair from my face. "Merry Christmas, little elf."

EPILOGUE
"That's…archaic."

ONE YEAR LATER

NEL

"**O**kay guys, that is my Christmas day makeup. I hope you liked this tutorial and make use of it tomorrow. I wish you all a fabulous Christmas and I'll be back in the New Year with some more posing tips and regular shoot updates. A lot of you have been asking for it, so I will be doing another couples posing video; yes, my boyfriend will be helping out. No, he will not be shirtless. Although, he is very flattered by all your requests. Merry Christmas everyone, I'll see you next year."

I wave at the screen of my phone and stop the recording. I'll edit and post it first thing in the morning, Christmas Eve. Checking myself in the mirror, I'm happy with the makeup look I've created, so I turn off my ring light and pack away my makeup case.

"I'm your boyfriend now?" Jake says, sat up against the headboard, he's already dressed and ready to go. He crosses his arms over his chest and tries for a glare but the smirk on his lips is reflected in his eyes.

"I can't exactly tell them lot until I've told Harry now, can I?" I purse my lips at him.

"But you're not posting it until tomorrow." He stands and makes his way over to me at the small dresser of the hotel room.

163

"No," I agree slowly as he leans on the armrests either side of me, caging me in.

"I'm not your boyfriend anymore, little elf."

"Oh, I'm little elf again now, am I?" I smirk.

"You're always little elf to me, *fiancé*."

I look down at the simple solitaire on my ring finger and bite my lip to keep in my heady excitement.

"Just think, this time next year, you'll be Mrs. Partridge."

I throw my head back and laugh. "You think we'll be able to plan and pay for a wedding in twelve months?"

"No?"

"No," I shake my head and peck his lips. "Come on, Mr. Partridge, we've got to get to Harry and Lisa's by seven. I read the itinerary this year and won't waste my revision by being late."

"Fine," he concedes. "You do know that Harry probably knows we're engaged, right?"

"How would he know?"

"I asked his permission."

I blink at him. "That's…archaic."

He smiles, all Elvis and charm. "Maybe, but if your dad was still around, he would have appreciated being asked, so I did the next best thing."

My eyes sting and I swallow back the tears. "That's sweet, Jake. That's really sweet."

"Come on, Mrs. Partridge, let's get to your brother's. I want to see baby Mary before she goes to bed."

I roll my eyes but fall in love with him a little more every time he fawns over my niece. To be fair, she is pretty cute.

Harry and Lisa are all smiles as they greet us at the door, looking cool, calm, and relaxed, as though they aren't just embarking on a four-day extravaganza, hosting Christmas for

164

twenty-one people! That's right, tomorrow Jake's parents, sister, brother-in-law, niece, and nephew arrive as well as everyone from last year. Lisa is perfectly made up, not so much as a crease in her pretty holly and ivy dress.

"You're here!" She wraps me in a warm hug, and I squeeze her back. "You look fantastic."

"So do you," I smile at her then give my brother a peck on the cheek.

We pass them into the porch and deposit our coats and shoes. When we look back at them, they both look at us with palpable excitement and expectation.

"What?" I ask, nervously.

"Have you got any news for us?" Harry asks, practically bouncing on his feet. His eyes flicking quickly to my hand.

I roll my eyes. "You couldn't have let me get a drink first?" But I hold up my hand and show them my ring. Lisa squeals and jumps up and down, clapping her hands. Harry slumps slightly, looking to the ceiling as if saying, *finally*.

We hug and kiss and cry and laugh until Harry ushers me into the living room where everyone is waiting and urges me to say it out loud.

"Jake and I are engaged."

Everyone cheers so loudly that baby Mary bursts into surprised tears and we all coo over her to turn her frown upside down. Rhiannon hugs me, her new baby bump just starting to show and when Freddie and Margot see me, they come over to say hello. They recognise me now after seeing them throughout the year at birthday celebrations and parties. I'm so happy that they have warmed to me as much as they have Jake.

"Nelly-Belly!" Lucas charges into me, squeezing my waist so tight I can barely breathe. Harry stopped using my childhood nickname as soon as I asked him to, but I couldn't bring myself to ask Lucas to, it seems so much more affectionate from him.

"Hey, buddy."

"Hi Aunty Nels-Bells."

"Hi Ozzy."

"You and Uncle Jake are going to get married?" Lucas asks.

"Yep, what do you think about that?"

"So cool," Lucas says. "I was a pageboy for Mummy's friend's wedding and I was really good at it, just so you know."

"We'll bare that in mind, buddy." Jake chuckles as he comes up to my side, handing me a cocktail as he kisses my cheek.

The boys scurry back to play with their little sister and the room around us fills with the sound of chatter and laughter.

"I love you, Jake Partridge."

"I love you too, little elf."

AUTHOR'S NOTE

Well, what can I say? Thank you for reading my Christmas story. I am always so humbled when people choose to pick up my book, let alone actually read it! You are one of my favourite people ever for taking a chance on a lil' indie author like me. If you enjoyed this, please do consider leaving a review on Goodreads or Amazon.

If you're interested in reading more of my work, please check out:

- Take Me Home – a billionaire New York CEO meets British country girl and after ten years of marriage a change of scenery is required.
- Their Starlight – An MMFM dark Mafia Romance, standalone but the first in what will be a four-part series.

If you would like to keep up to date with new releases and be first to sign up for future ARCs, please check out my website, www.hrlloyd.co.uk and sign up to my reader list.

Follow me on:
- TikTok - @han_ro_ll
- Instagram – @author_h.r.lloyd

ACKNOWLEDGEMENTS

Kerri D, my lovely editor, thank you for all your help and for sticking with me when I went off on tangents asking about things that had nothing to do with this book. I am so glad I now know how bed sizes work in America.

Hannah and Kirsty, thank you for being my Guinea pigs and reading bits when I send them to you. Your feedback is always so encouraging and I adore you both.

My Beta readers, Carley, Samantha, Caitlin, Jyoti and Haley, thank you so much for your help in moulding and shaping this into the story it is today. Your feedback was so helpful and I appreciate you.

Finally, thank you to my wonderful TikTok followers. I have found my people and without you I wouldn't have rediscovered my love for reading or had the push I needed to start taking my writing seriously.

Printed in Great Britain
by Amazon

30969298R00099